Susan Warner

Opportunities

A sequel to what she could

Susan Warner

Opportunities
A sequel to what she could

ISBN/EAN: 9783337156497

Printed in Europe, USA, Canada, Australia, Japan

Cover: Foto ©Andreas Hilbeck / pixelio.de

More available books at **www.hansebooks.com**

OPPORTUNITIES.

A SEQUEL TO "WHAT SHE COULD."

BY

THE AUTHOR OF
"THE WIDE WIDE WORLD."

"Whatsoever thy hand findeth to do, do it." — ECC. ix. 10.

NEW YORK:
ROBERT CARTER AND BROTHERS,
530, BROADWAY.
1871.

CAMBRIDGE:

PRESS OF JOHN WILSON AND SON.

OPPORTUNITIES.

CHAPTER I.

IT was the morning after that Sunday when Matilda had been baptized. The girls came down to prepare breakfast as usual; Maria in a very unsettled humour. She was cloudy and captious to a degree that Matilda could not understand. The kitchen was hot; the butter was soft; the milk was turned; the bread was dry. All things went wrong.

"It is no wonder the bread is dry," said Matilda; "it has been baked ever since last Friday."

"Thursday. I didn't say it was a wonder.

CAMBRIDGE:

PRESS OF JOHN WILSON AND SON.

OPPORTUNITIES.

CHAPTER I.

IT was the morning after that Sunday when Matilda had been baptized. The girls came down to prepare breakfast as usual; Maria in a very unsettled humour. She was cloudy and captious to a degree that Matilda could not understand. The kitchen was hot; the butter was soft; the milk was turned; the bread was dry. All things went wrong.

"It is no wonder the bread is dry," said Matilda; "it has been baked ever since last Friday."

"Thursday. I didn't say it was a wonder.

Aunt Candy *will* have the bread dry.   I hate it!"

" And it is no wonder the butter is soft, if you keep it up here in the kitchen.   The kitchen must be hot, with this hot stove. But the milkman will be along directly."

" No, he won't.   We always have to wait for him ; or take the old milk.   And I can't be bothered to keep the butter down cellar and be running for it fifty times in an hour.   I have enough to do as it is.   Whatever possessed aunt Erminia to want corn bread this morning!"

" Does she want corn bread ? "

" Yes."

" Well, corn bread is nice. I am glad of it."

" You wouldn't be glad if you had to make it.   There! I knew it would be so.   There isn't a speck of soda.   Put on your bonnet, Matilda, and run round to Mr. Sample's and get some soda, will you? — and be quick. We shall be late, and then there will be a row."

" There won't be a *row*, Maria. Aunt Candy is always quiet."   .

" I wish she wouldn't, then. I hate people who are always quiet. I would rather they would flare out now and then. It's safer."

" For what? *Safer*, Maria ? "

" Do go along and get your soda!" exclaimed Maria. "Do you think it will be safe to be late with breakfast ? "

Maria was so evidently out of order this morning, that her sister thought the best way was to let her alone; only she asked, " Aren't you well, Maria? " and got a sharp answer; then she went out.

It was a delicious spring morning. The air stirred in her face its soft and glad breaths of sweetness; the sunlight was the very essence of promise; the village and the green trees, now out in leaf, shone and basked in the fair day. It was better than breakfast, to be out in the air. Matilda went round the corner, into Butternut street, and made for Mr. Sample's grocery store, every step being a delight. Why could not the inside world be as pleasant as. the outside? Matilda was musing and wishing, when just before she reached Mr. Sample's door, she saw what made her forget everything else; even the mischievous little boy who belonged to Mrs. Dow. What was he doing here in Butternut street? Matilda's steps slackened. The boy knew her, for he looked and then grinned, and then bringing a finger alongside of his nose in a peculiar and mysterious expressiveness, he repeated his old words, —

" Ain't you green ? "

" I suppose so," said Matilda. " I dare say I am. What then ? Green is not the worst colour."

The boy looked at her, a little confounded.

" If you would come to Sunday school," Matilda went on, " *you* would be a better colour than you are, — by and by."

" What colour be I ? " said the boy.

" You'd be a better colour," said Matilda. " Just come and see."

"I ain't green," the boy remonstrated.

Matilda passed on, went into Mr. Sample's and got her soda. She had a few cents of change. A thought came into her head. Peeping out, she saw that Mrs. Dow's boy was still lingering where she had left him. Immediately Matilda requested to have the worth of those cents in sugared almonds; and with her little packages went into the street again. The boy eyed her.

"What is your name?" said Matilda.

"Hain't got none."

"Yes, you have. What does your mother call you at home?"

"She calls me — the worst of all her plagues," said the fellow, grinning.

"No, no; but when she calls you from somewhere — what does she call you?"

"She calls me out of the garding, and down from the attic."

"Look here," said Matilda, shewing a sugarplum; "I'll give you that, if you will tell me."

The boy eyed it, and her, and finally said,—

" Lem."

" Your name is Lem ? "

He nodded.

" There, Lem, is a sugarplum for you. Now if you'll come to Sunday school next Sunday, and stay and behave yourself, I'll give you three more."

" Three more ? " said the boy.

" Yes.   Now come, and you'll like it."

And Matilda sped home with her soda.

" I should think you had been making the soda," said Maria ; " you have been long enough.   What kept you ? "

" How *do* they make soda, I wonder ? " said Matilda, looking at it.   " Do you know, Maria ? "

" I have enough to do to know how to get breakfast.   Tilly, run and grind the coffee and make it,— quick, will you ? now I am in a hurry."

Matilda thought Maria *might* have done it

herself, while she was waiting for the soda. But she said nothing of that. In ten minutes more the coffee was made, the corn bread was ready, and the ladies came down.

Matilda was in a mood as gentle as the morning, and almost as cloudless. Her morning's work and walk and the meeting with Lem Dow had given her an appetite; and the work of the night before had left a harmony in her spirit, as if sweet music were sounding there. Her little face was thus like the very morning itself, shining with the fair shining of inward beauty; in contrast with all the other faces at the table. For Clarissa's features were coldly handsome and calm; Mrs. Candy's were set and purposeful; and poor Maria's were sadly clouded and out of humour. Matilda took little heed of them all; she was thinking of Lemuel Dow.

"Matilda," said her aunt suddenly, — "I wish you to come to me every morning to read. A person who has taken the step you took last night, is no longer a child, but deserves to be treated as a woman. It is necessary that you should fit yourself for a woman's place. Come to me at ten o'clock. I will have you read to me some books that will make you better understand the things you have taken upon you, and the things you have done."

"Why I am a child yet, aunt Candy," Matilda answered in some dismay.

"You think so, do you?"

"Yes, ma'am, — I feel so; and I *am*."

"I thought you considered yourself more than a child. But you have assumed a woman's place, and it is now necessary that you should be fitted for it. *I* think the best way is to get the preparation first; but in your church, it seems, they prefer the other course. You are under my care in the house, at any rate, and I shall do my duty by you."

"I do not understand you, aunt Candy," Matilda spoke, quite bewildered.

"No, my dear, I suppose not. That is

just what I think so objectionable. But we will do what we can to remedy it."

"What do you want to prepare me for, aunt Erminia?"

"For your position, my dear, as a member of the church. That is not a child's position. You have placed yourself in it; and now the question is how to enable you to maintain it properly. I cannot treat you as a child any longer."

Matilda wondered very much how she was to be treated. However, silence seemed the wisest plan at present.

"I suppose *I* am a child still," remarked Maria.

"I have never observed anything inconsistent with that supposition, my dear," her aunt serenely answered.

"And if I had been baptized last night, you would have more respect for me," went on poor Maria.

"My respect is not wholly dependent on forms, my dear. If it had been done in a proper way, of course, things would be different from what they are. I *should* have more respect for you."

" Clarissa has done it in a proper way, I suppose ? "

" When she was of a proper age, — yes; certainly."

" And then, what did she promise ? All that they promised last night ? "

" The vows are much the same."

" Well, people ought not to make vows till they are ready to keep them — ought they ? "

" Certainly they should not."

" Well " —

" My dear, it is a very bad habit to begin every sentence with a ' well.' You do it constantly."

" Well, aunt Candy " —

" There ! " exclaimed Clarissa. " Again."

" Well, I don't care," said Maria. " I can't help it. I don't know when I do it. I was going to ask, — and you put everything out of my head. — Aunt Candy, do you think Clarissa has given up, really, the pomps and vanities and all that, you know? She spent twenty-four dollars, I heard her say, on the trimming of that muslin dress; and she bought a parasol the other day for ten dollars, when one for three would have done perfectly well; and she pays always twelve dollars for her boots, twelve and ten dollars; when she could get nice ones for four and five. Now what's that?"

"It's impertinence," said Clarissa. "And untruth; for the four and five dollar boots hurt my feet."

"They are *exactly* the same," said Maria; "except the kid and the trimming and the beautiful making."

"Very well," said Clarissa, "I have a right to wear comfortable shoes, if I can get them."

"Then you have a right to pomps and vanities," returned Maria; "but I say you *haven't* a right, after you have declared and sworn you would have nothing to do with them."

" Mamma," said Clarissa, but with heightened colour, — " Is this a child?"

" After the Shadywalk pattern," Mrs. Candy answered.

" Girls in Shadywalk have a *little* sense, when they get to be as old as sixteen," Maria went on. " Where you have been, perhaps they do not grow up so fast."

. " People would put weights on their heads if they did," said Clarissa.

" It doesn't matter," said Maria. " You can imagine that I am as old as you are; and I say, that it is more respectable not to make promises and vows than to make them and not keep them."

" Do not answer her, my dear," said Mrs. Candy.

" And that is the reason why I have *not* been baptized, or whatever you call it " —

" I never said so, Maria," said her aunt. " The two things are not the same."

" Imagine it! " said Clarissa.

" Well, you said just now — I don't know what you said! — but you said at any rate that if it had been done in a proper way, you would think more of me; and *I* say, that it is better not to make vows till you are ready to keep them. I am not ready to give up dancing; and I would have expensive hats and dresses, and feathers, and watches, and chains, and everything pretty that money can buy, if I had the money; and I like them; and I want them."

" I have not given up dancing," said Clarissa.

" Nor other things either," retorted Maria ; " but they are pomps and vanities. That is what I say. You promised you would have nothing to do with them."

" Mamma ! " said Clarissa appealingly.

" Yes, my dear," said her mother. " The amount of ignorance in Maria's words discourages me from trying to answer them."

" Ignorance and superstition, mamma."

" And superstition," — said Mrs. Candy.

" Matilda thinks just the same way," Clarissa went on, meeting the broad open, astonished eyes of the little girl.

" Of course," said Mrs. Candy. " Matilda is too much a child to exercise her own judgment on these matters. She just takes what has been told her."

" Have you given up dancing too, Tilly ? " Clarissa went on.

" I have never thought about it, cousin Clarissa."

. " Matilda all over!" exclaimed the young lady. " She has not thought about it, mamma. When she thinks about it, she will know what her part is."

" Very well," said Mrs. Candy. " She might do worse."

" I suppose you think I can't think," said poor Maria.

" No, my dear; I only think you have not begun yet to use your power in that direction. When you do, you will see things differently At least I hope so."

" It would take a good deal of thinking, to make me see that giving up the world and going into it were the same thing," said Maria. " And I don't mean to promise to do it till I'm ready."

" Mamma, this is not very pleasant," said Clarissa.

" No, my dear. We will leave the field to Maria. Come to me at ten o'clock, Matilda."

The two ladies filed off upstairs, and Maria sat down to cry. Matilda began to clear the table, going softly back and forth between the basement and the kitchen as if there were trouble in the house. Maria sobbed.

" Ain't they mean ! " she exclaimed, starting up at length. Matilda was busy going in and out, and said nothing.

" Matilda ! Why don't you speak ? I say, ain't they mean ? "

" There's no use in talking so, Maria," said her little sister, looking sorrowful.

" Yes, there is. People ought to hear the truth."

" But if you know what is right, why don't you *do* it, Maria ? "

" I do — as well as I can."

" But Maria ! — I mean, about what you were saying; giving up whatever is not right."

" Things are right for other people, that are not right for members of the church. That's why I want to wait awhile.　I am not ready."

" But Maria — what makes them right for other people ? "

" They have not promised anything about them.　Clarissa has *promised*, and she don't do."

" You have not promised."

" No, of course I haven't."

" But if they are right things, Maria, why *should* you, or anybody, promise not to have anything to do with them ? "

" O you are too wise, Matilda ! " her sister answered impatiently.　" There is no need for you to go to read with aunt Candy; you know everything already."

The rest of the morning was very silent between the sisters, till it came to the time for Matilda to present herself in her aunt's room. There meanwhile a consultation had been held.

"Mamma, that girl is getting unendurable."

"Must wait a little while, my dear."

"What will you do with her then?"

"Something. I can send her to school, at any rate."

"But the expense, mamma?"

"It is not much, at the district school. That is where she has been going

"Matilda too?"

"I suppose that will be the best place. I am not sure about sending Matilda. She's a fine child."

"She will be handsome, mamma."

"She is very graceful now. She has a singular manner."

"But she is spoiled, mamma!"

"I shall un-spoil her. Tilly is very young yet, and she has not had enough to do. I shall give her something else to think of, and get these absurdities out of her head. She just wants something to do."

"Mamma, she is not an easy child to influence. She says so little and keeps her own counsel. I think you don't know her."

"I never saw the child yet that was a match for me," said Mrs. Candy complacently. "I like best one that has some stuff in her. Maria is a wet sponge; you can squeeze her dry in a minute; no character, no substance. Matilda is different. I should like to keep Tilly."

"If you could keep her out of Mr. Richmond's influence, mamma, it would be a help. That church ruins her. She will be fit for nothing."

"I will take the nonsense out of her," said Mrs. Candy. "I cannot take her out of the church; while we remain here, for that would raise a hue and cry; but I will do as well. Here she comes."

A little soft knock at the door was followed

by the little girl herself; looking demure and sweet, after her fashion lately. It used to be arch and sweet. But Matilda had been very sober since her mother's death. The room into which she came had an air now very unlike all the rest of the house. Mrs. Englefield's modest preparations for the comfort of her guests were quite overlaid and lost sight of. It was as if some fairy had shaken her hand over the room and let fall pleasant things everywhere. On the Marseilles quilt a gorgeous silk coverlet lay folded. On the dressing table a confusion of vases and bottles, in coloured glass and painted china, were mixed up with combs and brushes and fans and watch pockets and taper stands. The table in the middle of the floor was heaped with elegant books and trinkets and work-boxes and writing implements; and book stands and book shelves were about, and soft foot cushions were dropped on the carpet, and easy arm chairs stood conveniently, and some faint perfume breathed all through

the room.   Mrs. Candy was in one arm chair
and Clarissa in another.

Matilda was bidden to take a cricket, which
she privately resented, and then her aunt
placed in her hands a largish volume and
pointed her to the page where she was to
begin.   Glancing up and down, at the top of
the page and the beginning of the book,
Matilda found it was a treatise, or a collection
of advices, for the instruction of persons about
to be received into the church.   Not a little
dismayed by this discovery, no less than by
the heavy look of the pages, Matilda however
began her reading.   It was dragging work,
as she expected.   Her thoughts wandered.
What could her aunt think she wanted with
this, when she had Mr. Richmond's instruc-
tions?   What could these ponderous reason-
ings be expected to add to his words?   The
immediate effect of them certainly was not
salutary to Matilda's mind.

"My dear, you do not read so well as
usual," her aunt said at length.

Matilda paused, glad to stop even for a little.

"Your sentences come heavily from your tongue."

"Yes. They *are* heavy, aunt Candy."

"My dear! Those are the words of the Rev. Benjamin Orderly — a very famous writer, and loved by all good people. Those are excellent words that you have been reading."

Matilda said nothing further.

"Did you understand them?"

"They did not interest me, aunt Candy."

"My dear, they ought to interest one who has just taken such a step as you have taken."

Matilda wondered privately whether being baptized ought properly to have any effect to change the natural taste and value of things; but she did not answer.

"You understood what you read, did you?"

Matilda coloured a little.

"Aunt Candy, it was not interesting, and I did not think about it."

Mrs. Candy drew the book severely from Matilda's hand.

"After taking such a step as you took last night, you ought to *try* to be interested, if it were only for consistency's sake. Do you see that you were hasty? A person who does not care about the privileges and duties of church membership most certainly ought not to be a church member."

"But aunt Candy, I do care," said Matilda.

"So it seems."

"I care about it as the Bible speaks of it; and as Mr. Richmond talks about it."

"You are very fond of Mr. Richmond, I know."

Matilda added nothing to that, and there was a pause.

"Do you want anything more of me, aunt Candy?"

"Yes. I want to teach you something useful. Here are a quantity of stockings of yours that need mending. I am going to shew you how to mend them. Go and get your work-box and bring it here."

"Couldn't you tell me what you want me to do, aunt Candy, and let me go and do it where Maria is?"

"No. Maria is busy. And I have got to take a good deal of pains to teach you, Tilly, what I want you to know. Go fetch your box and work things."

Matilda slowly went. It was so pleasant to be out of that perfumed room and out of sight of the Rev. Mr. Orderly's writings. She lingered in the passages; looked over the balusters and listened, hoping that by some happy chance Maria might make some demand upon her. None came; the house was still; and Matilda had to go back to her aunt. She felt like a prisoner.

"Now I suppose you have no darning cotton," said Mrs. Candy. "Here is a needleful. Thread it, and then I will shew you what next."

" This is three or four needlefuls, aunt Candy. I will break it. I cannot sew with such a thread."

" Stop. Yes, you can. Don't break it. I will shew you. Thread your needle."

" I haven't one big enough."

That want was supplied.

" Now you shall begin with running this heel," said Mrs. Candy. " See, you shall put this marble egg into the stocking, to darn upon. Now look here. You begin down here, at the middle, so, — and take up only one thread at a stitch, do you see? and skip so many threads each time," —

" But there is no hole there, aunt Erminia."

" I know that.   Heels should always be run before they come to holes. There are half-a-dozen heels here, I should think, that require to be run. Now do you see how I do it? You may take the stocking, and when you have darned a few rows, come and let me see how you get on."

Matilda in a small fit of despair took the

stocking to a little distance and sat down to
work. The marble egg was heavy to hold.
It took a long while to go up one side of the
heel and down the other. She was tired of
sitting under constraint and so still. And
her aunt Candy seemed like a jailer, and that
perfumed room like a prison. The quicker
her work could be done, the better for her.
So Matilda reflected, and her needle went
accordingly.

"I have done it, aunt Erminia," she pro-
claimed at last.

"Done the heel?"

"Yes, ma'am."

"You cannot possibly. Come here and let
me look at it. Why, of course! That is not
done as I shewed you, Tilly; these rows of
darning should be close together, one stitch
just in the middle between two other stitches;
you have just gone straggling over the whole
heel. That will have to come all out."

"But there is no hole in it," said Matilda.

"Always darn *before* the holes come. That

will not do. You must pick it all out,
Tilly."

" Now ? " said Matilda despairingly.

" Certainly, now. You make yourself
trouble in that way. I am sorry. Pick it
all neatly out."

Matilda went at it impatiently ; tugged at
the thread ; pulled the heel of her stocking
into a very intricate drawn-up state ; then had
to smooth it out again with difficulty.

" This is very hard to come out," she said.

" Yes, it is bad picking," said her aunt
composedly.

Matilda was very impatient and very weary
besides.   However, work did it, in time.

" Now see if you can do it better," said
Mrs. Candy.

" *Now*, aunt Erminia ?"

" Certainly.   It is your own fault that you
have made such a business of it.   You should
have done as I told you."

" But I am *very* tired."

" I dare say you are."

Matilda was very much in the mind to cry; but that would not have mended matters, and would have hurt her pride besides. She went earnestly to work with her darning needle instead. She could use it nicely, she found, with giving pains and time enough. But it took a great while to do a little. Up one side and down the other; then up that side and down the first; threading long double needle-fuls, and having them used up with great rapidity; Matilda seemed to grow into a darning machine. She was very still; only a deep drawn long breath now and then heaved her little breast. Impatience faded however, and a sort of dulness crept over her. At last she became very tired, so tired that pride gave way and she said so.

Mrs. Candy remarked that she was sorry.

"Aunt Candy, I think Maria may want me by this time."

"Yes. *That* is of no consequence."

"Maria has got no one to help her."

"She will not hurt herself," Clarissa observed.

"Aunt Erminia, wouldn't you just as lieve I should finish this by and by?"

"I will think of that," said her aunt. "All you have to do, is to work on."

"I am very tired of it!"

"That is not a reason for stopping, my dear. Rather the contrary. One must learn to do things after one is tired. That is a lesson I learned a great while ago."

"I cannot work so well or so fast, when I am tired," said Matilda.

"And I cannot work at all while you are talking to me."

Matilda's slow fingers drew the needle in and out for some time longer. Then to her great joy, the dinner bell rang.

"What does Maria mean?" said Mrs. Candy looking at her watch. "It wants an hour of dinner time. Run and see what it is, Matilda."

Matilda ran downstairs.

" Do you think I have five pairs of hands ? " inquired Maria indignantly. " It is nice for you to be playing upstairs, and I working as hard as I can in the kitchen ! I won't stand this, I can tell you."

" Playing ! " echoed Matilda. " Well, Maria, what do you want done ? "

" Look and see. You have eyes. About everything is to be done. There's the castors to put in order, and the lettuce to get ready — I wish lettuce wouldn't grow ! — and the table to set, and the sauce to make for the pudding. Now hurry."

It was absolutely better than play, to fly about and do all these things, after the confinement of darning stockings. Matilda's glee equalled Maria's discomfiture. Only, when it was all done and the dinner ready, Matilda stood still to think. " I am sorry I was so impatient this morning upstairs," she said to herself.

CHAPTER II.

MATILDA'S spirits were not quite used up by the morning's experience, for after dinner she put on her bonnet and took her Bible and set off on an expedition, without asking leave of anybody. She was bent upon getting to Lilac lane. "If I do not get there to-day, I don't know when I shall," she said to herself. "There is no telling what aunt Candy will do."

She got there without any difficulty. It was an overcast Aprilish day, with low clouds, and now and then a drop of rain falling. Matilda did not care for that. It was all the pleasanter walking. Lilac lane was at some distance from home, and the sun had a good deal of power on sunny days now. The mud was all gone by this time; in its place a thick

groundwork of dust. Winter frost was re-
placed by soft spring air; but that gave a
chance for the lane odours to come out; not
the fragrance of hawthorn and primrose by
any means. Nor any such pleasant sight to
be seen. Poor, straggling, forlorn houses;
broken fences, or no courtyards at all; thick
dust, and no footway; garbage and ashes and
bones, but never even so much as a green
potato patch to greet the eye, much less a
rose or a pink; an iron shop, and a livery
stable at the entrance of the lane seeming
dignified and elegant buildings by comparison
with what came afterwards. Few living
things were abroad; a boy or two, and two
or three babies making discomposure in the
dust, were about all. Matilda wondered if
every one of those houses did not need to have
the message carried to them? Where was
she to begin?

"Does Mrs. Eldridge live in this house,
or in that?" Matilda asked a boy in her
way.

" In nary one."

" Where *does* she live ? "

" Old Sally Eldridge ? Sam's grand-mother ? "

" I don't know anything about Sam," said Matilda. " She lives alone."

" Well, *she* lives alone. That's her door yonder— where the cat sits."

" Thank you." Matilda thought to ask if the boy went to Sunday school; but she felt as if all the force she had would be wanted to carry her through the visit to Mrs. Eldridge. It was a forlorn looking doorway; the upper half of the door swinging partly open; the cottage dropping down on one side, as if it was tired of the years when it had stood up ; not a speck of paint to be seen anywhere, and little bare broken windows, not even patched with rags. Matilda walked up to the door and knocked, sorely appalled at the view she got through the half open doorway. No answer. She knocked again. Then a weak, " Who is it ? "

Matilda let herself in. There was a worn and torn rag carpet; an unswept floor; boards and walls that had not known the touch of water or soap in many, many months; a rusty little stove with no fire in it; and a poor old woman, who looked in all respects like her surroundings; worn and torn and dusty and unwashed and neglected. To her Matilda turned, with a great sinking of heart. What could *she* do?

"Who's here?" said the old woman, who did not seem to have her sight clear.

"Matilda Englefield."

"I don't know no such a person."

"Maybe you would like to know me," said Matilda. "I am come to see you."

"What fur? I hain't sent for nobody. Who told you to come?"

"No, I know you didn't. But I wanted to come and see you, Mrs. Eldridge."

"What fur? You're a little gal, bain't you?"

"Yes ma'am; and I thought maybe you

would like to have me read a chapter in the Bible to you."

" A *what?* " said the old woman with strong emphasis.

" A chapter in the Bible. I thought — perhaps you couldn't see to read it yourself."

" Read?" said the old creature. " Never could. I never could see to read, for I never knowed how. No, I never knowed how; I didn't."

" You would like to hear reading, now, wouldn't you? I came to read to you a chapter — if you'll let me — out of the Bible."

" A chapter?" the old woman repeated — " what's a chapter now? It's no odds; 'taint bread, nor 'taint 'baccy."

" No, it is not tobacco," said Matilda; " but it is better than tobacco."

" Couldn't ye get me some 'baccy, now?" said the old woman, as if with a sudden thought. But Matilda did not see her way clear to that; and the hope failing, the failure of everything seemed to be expressed in a long-drawn "heigh-ho!" which ran wearily down all the notes of the gamut. Matilda felt she was not getting on. The place and the woman were inexpressibly forlorn to her.

"Who sent ye fur to come here?" was next asked.

"Nobody sent me."

"What fur did ye come?"

"I thought you would like to hear a little reading."

"'Taint a song, is it? I used fur to hear songs oncet; they don't sing songs in this village. They sells good 'baccy, though. Heigh-ho!"

Matilda grew desperate. She was not making any headway. As a last expedient, she opened her book, plunged into the work, and gave in the hearing of Mrs. Eldridge a few of its wonderful sentences. Maybe those words would reach her, thought Matilda. She read slowly the twenty-third psalm, and then went back to the opening verse and read it again.

"' The Lord is my shepherd; I shall not want.' "

Mrs. Eldridge had been very still.

" A shepherd," she repeated, when Matilda had stopped; — " he used fur to be a shepherd."

Matilda wondered very much what the old lady was thinking of. Her next words made it clearer.

" He kept sheep fur Mr. — Mr. — him they called the Judge; I don't mind who he was. He kept sheep for him, he did."

" Judge Brockenhurst? "

" That was it — I can't speak his name; he kept his sheep. It was a big place."

" Yes, I know Judge Brockenhurst's place," said Matilda; " he has a great many sheep. *Who* kept them? ".

" He did, dear. My old man. He kept 'em. It's long sen."

" Well, didn't he take good care of them, the sheep? "

" My old man? Ay, did he. There warn't

no better a shepherd in the country. He took care of 'em. The Judge sot a great deal by him."

" How did he take care of them ?" Matilda asked.

" O I don' know. He watched 'em, and he took 'em round, and he didn't let no harm happen to 'em. He didn't."

" Well, this I read was about the Good Shepherd and *his* sheep. He takes care of them, too. Don't you think the Lord Jesus takes care of his sheep ?"

" He don't take no care o' me," said the poor old woman. " There ain't no care took o' me anywheres, — neither in heaven nor in earth. No, there ain't."

" But are you one of his sheep ?" said Matilda doubtfully.

" Eh ?" said the woman, pricking up her ears, as it were.

" Are you one of the Lord's sheep, Mrs. Eldridge ? "

" Am I one of 'em? I'm poor enough fur

to be took care of; I am.   And there ain't
no care took o' me.   Neither in heaven nor
on earth.   No, there ain't."

"But are you one of his sheep?" Matilda
persisted.   "His sheep follow him.   Did you
ever do that, ma'am?   Were you ever a servant of the Lord Jesus?"

"A servant?   I warn't no servant, nowheres," was the answer.   "I had no need to
do that.   We was 'spectable folks, and we
had our own home and lived in it, we did.
I warn't never no servant o' nobody."

"But we all ought to be God's servants,"
said Matilda.

"Eh? — I hain't done no harm, I hain't.
Nobody never said as I done 'em no
harm."

"But the servants of Jesus love him and
obey him and do what he says," Matilda
repeated, growing eager.   "They do just
what he says; and they love him, and they
love everybody, because he gives them new
hearts."

"I don't know as he never give me noth-ing," said Mrs. Eldridge.

"Did you ever ask him for a new heart? and did you ever try to please him? Then you would be one of his sheep, and he would take care of you."

"Nobody takes no care o' me," said the poor woman stolidly.

"Listen," said Matilda. "This is what he says, —

"'I am the good shepherd; the good shep-herd giveth his life for the sheep.' He cared so much for you as that. 'I am the good shepherd, and know my sheep, and am known of mine. As the Father knoweth me, even so know I the Father: and I lay down my life for the sheep.'"

"He cared so much for you as that. He died that you might be forgiven and live. Don't say he didn't care?"

"I didn't know as he'd never done nothing fur me," said Mrs. Eldridge.

"He did that. Listen, now, please."

" 'My sheep hear my voice, and I know them, and they follow me: and I give unto them eternal life; and they shall never perish, neither shall any pluck them out of my hand. My Father, which gave them me, is greater than all; and none is able to pluck them out of my Father's hand. I and my Father are one.' "

Matilda lifted her head and sought, in the faded blue eye over against her, if she could find any response to these words. She fancied there was a quieter thoughtfulness in it.

" That has a good sound," was the old woman's comment, uttered presently. " But I'm old now, and I can't do nothing; and there ain't nobody to take care o' me. There ain't."

Matilda glanced over the desolate room. It was dusty, dirty, neglected, and poverty stricken. What if *she* had been sent to " take care " of Mrs. Eldridge ? The thought was exceedingly disagreeable ; but once come, she could not get rid of it.

" What do you want, Mrs. Eldridge ? " she asked at length.

" I don't want no more readin'. But it has a good sound — a good sound."

" What would you like to have somebody do for you ? not reading."

" There was folks as cared fur me," said the old woman. " There ain't none no more. No more. There ain't no one as cares."

" But if there *was* some one — what would you tell her to do for you ? — now, to-day ? "

" Any one as cared would know," said Mrs. Eldridge. " There's 'most all to do. 'Spect I'd have a cup o' tea for my supper — 'spect I would."

" Don't you have tea ? Won't you have it to-night ? "

The feeble eye looked over at the little rusty stove.

" There ain't no fire," she said; " nor noth-ing to make fire; it's cold; and there ain't nobody to go out and get it fur me — I can't go pick up sticks no more. An' if I had the fire, there ain't no tea.　There ain't no one as cares."

" But what will you have then ? " said Matilda.　" What do you have for supper ? "

" Go and look," said Mrs. Eldridge, turning her head towards a corner cupboard the doors of which stood a little open.　" If there's anything, it's there; if it ain't all eat up."

Matilda hesitated; then thought she had better know the state of things, since she had leave; and crossed to the cupboard door.　It was a problem with her how to open it; so long, long it was since anything clean had touched the place; she made the end of her glove finger do duty and pulled the cupboard leaves open.

She never forgot what she saw there, nor the story of lonely and desolate life which it told.　Two cups and saucers, one standing in a back corner, unused and full of cobwebs, the other cracked, soiled, grimy and full of flies.　Something had been in it; what, Matilda could not examine.　On the bare shelf lay a half loaf of bread, pretty dry, with a knife alongside. A plate of broken meat, also full of flies, and looking, Matilda thought, fit for the flies alone, was there; a cup half full of salt; an empty vinegar cruet, an old shawl, ditto hood; a pitcher with no water; an old muslin cap, half soiled; a faded bit of ribband, and a morsel of cheese flanked by a bitten piece of gingerbread. Matilda came back, sick at heart.

"Where do you sleep, Mrs. Eldridge? and who makes your bed? Or can you make it?"

"Sleep?" said the old woman. "Nobody cares. I sleep in yonder."

Matilda looked, doubted, finally crossed the room again and pushed a little inwards the door Mrs. Eldridge had looked at. She came back quickly. So close, so ill-smelling, so miserable to her nice senses, the room within was; with its huddled up bundle of dirty coverlets and the soiled bed under them on the floor. Not much of a bed either, and not much else in the room. A great burden was gathering on Matilda's heart and shoulders; the burden of the wants of her neighbour, and her own responsibilities.

The afternoon was now waning; what was to be done? Matilda tried to think that somebody would come in and do what she herself was very unwilling to do; but conscience reminded her that it was very unlikely. Did that neglected cupboard give much promise of kind attendance or faithful supply? or that rusty stove look like neighbourly care? But then Matilda pleaded to herself that she had her own work, and not much time; and that such a dirty place was very unfit for her nice little hands.

" Good bye, Mrs. Eldridge," she said, lingering. " I'll come and see you again."

" 'Taint a pleasant place to come to," said the old woman. " 'Taint a pleasant place fur nobody. And nobody comes to it. Nobody comes."

" I'll come though," said Matilda. She

could do so much as that, she thought. "Good bye. I must go home."

. She left the old woman and the house and began her walk. The lane, she observed, looked as if other houses and other people in it might be as ill off as those she had been visiting. " She is not worse than a number of others, I dare say," thought Matilda. " I could not visit them all, and I could not certainly take care of them all. It really makes little difference on the whole, whether or no I kindle Mrs. Eldridge's fire. It is delightful to get away from the place."

And then Matilda tried to think that in making her visit and reading to the old woman, she had really done a good deal; made a good afternoon's work. Nobody else had done even so much as that; not even anybody in all Shadywalk. The walk home was quite pleasant, under the soothing influence of these thoughts. Nevertheless a little secret point of uneasiness remained at Matilda's heart. She did not stop to look at it, until she and Maria went up to bed.   Then, as usual, while Maria got ready for sleep, Matilda knelt down before the table where her open Bible lay under the lamp, and there conscience met her.

And when conscience meets any one, it is the same thing as to say that the Lord meets him.

That was what Matilda felt this night. For her reading fell upon the story of the woman who brought the precious ointment for the head of Jesus and poured it upon his feet also; whom the Lord, when she was chidden, commended; saying, " Ye have the poor with you always, and whensoever ye will ye may do them good: but me ye have not always.   She hath done what she could." —

Had Matilda?   And these poor whom we have always with us, she recollected that in another place the Lord in a sort identifies himself with them, saying that what is done to his poor is done to himself.   Mrs. Eldridge was not indeed one of the Lord's children, but that did not help the matter. "For perhaps she will be," Matilda said to herself. And what if the Lord had sent Matilda there now to be his messenger? The success of the message might depend on the behaviour of the messenger. But above all it pressed upon Matilda's heart that she had not done what she *could;* and that in declining to make a fire in Mrs. Eldridge's rusty little stove and in shrinking from waiting upon her, she had lost a chance of waiting upon, perhaps, the Lord himself.

"And it was such a good chance," thought Matilda; "such a good afternoon; and there is no telling when I may get another. It was such a good opportunity. And I lost it."

The pain of a lost opportunity was something she had not counted upon. It pressed hard, and was not easy to get rid of. The disagreeableness of the place and the service faded into nothing before this pain. Matilda went to bed with a sore heart, resolving to watch for the very first chance to do what she had neglected to do this afternoon.

But Lilac lane looked very disagreeable to her thoughts the next day, and the sharp effect of the Bible words had faded somewhat.

" Maria," she said as they were washing up the dishes after breakfast, — " I wish you would help me in something."

" What? "

" Do you call yourself a member of the Band yet? "

" Of course I do. What do you ask for? "

" I did not know," said Matilda sighing. " You don't *do* the things promised in the covenant. I didn't know but you had given it all up."

" What don't I do? " inquired Maria fiercely.

" Don't be angry, please, Maria. I do not mean to make you angry."

" What don't I do, Matilda? "

" You know, the Covenant says, ' we stand

ready to do his will.' He has commanded that we should be baptized and join the church, and that we should follow him, — you know how, Maria. And you don't seem to like to do it."

" Is that all ? "

" That is all about that."

" Then, if you will mind your affairs, Matilda, I will try and mind mine. And I will be much obliged to you."

" Then you will not help me?"

" Help in what ?"

" There is a poor woman, Maria," said her little sister lowering · her voice, "a poor old woman, who has no one to take care of her, and hardly anything to live upon. She lives, you can't think how she lives! in the most miserable little house, dirty and all; and without fire or anybody to sweep her room or make her bed or make a cup of tea for her. If you would help me, we might do something to make her comfortable."

" Where is she ? "

" In Lilac lane."

" Have you been to see her ? "

" Yes."

" What do you think aunt Candy would say if she knew it ? "

" Will you help me, Maria ? "

" Help make her bed and sweep her room ?"

" Yes, and get her a cup of tea sometimes, and a clean supper."

" A clean supper!" exclaimed Maria. " Well! Yes, I guess I'll help you, when I have nothing of my own to do. When the dinner gets itself, and the house stays swept and dusted, and aunt ·Candy lives without cakes for breakfast."

Matilda was silent.

" But I'll tell you what, Matilda," said her sister, — " aunt Candy will never let you do this sort of work. You may as well give it up peaceably, and not worry yourself nor anybody else. She'll never let you go into Lilac lane — not to speak of getting dirty people's dinners. You may as well quit it.'

" Don't tell her, Maria."

" You'll tell her yourself, first thing," said Maria scornfully.

Matilda had to go upstairs soon to her reading in her aunt's room. It was even more unintelligible, the reading, this time than before; because Matilda's head was running so busily on something else.

" You do not read well, child," said her aunt.

" No, ma'am.   I do not understand it."

" But it is about what you have just done, Matilda.   It is about the ordinance of baptism, and the life proper to a person who has been received into the church.   You ought to understand that."

" I *do* understand it, in the Bible."

" What does the Bible say about it ? "

" It says, — ' My sheep hear my voice: and I know them, and they follow me.' "

" What do you mean by ' following Him ' ? "

" Why, living the sort of life he lived, and doing what he tells us to do."

"How do you propose to live the sort of life He lived? It's almost blasphemy."

"Why no, aunt Candy; he tells us to do it."

"Do what?"

"Live the sort of life he lived. He says we must follow him."

"Well how, for instance? In what?"

"You know how *he* lived," said Matilda. "He helped people, and he taught people, and he cured people; he was always doing good to people, and trying to make them good. Especially poor, miserable people, that nobody cared for."

"Trying to make them good!" said Mrs. Candy. "As if His omnipotence could not have made them good in a minute."

"Then why didn't he?" said Matilda simply. "It *sounds* as if he was trying to make them good."

"Well, child, — it's no use talking; I wish I had had the training of you earlier," said Mrs. Candy. "You are so prepossessed with ideas that border on fanaticism, that it is a hard matter to get you into right habits of thinking. Come here and take your darning."

So Matilda did. The darning was not wearisome at all to-day, so busy her thoughts were with the question of Mrs. Eldridge; how much or how little Matilda ought to do for her, how much she *could,* and what were the best arrangements to be set on foot. So intent she was on these questions, that the darning was done with the greatest patience, and therefore with the greatest success. Mrs. Candy and her daughter even looked at each other and smiled over the demure, thoughtful little face of the workwoman; and Matilda got praise for her work.

She had made up her mind meanwhile that "she hath done what she could" — should be her rule to go by. So as the afternoon was fair and Mrs. Candy and her daughter both gone to make a visit at some miles' distance, Matilda sallied forth.

" Did she give you leave ? " Maria asked, as she saw her sister getting ready.

" No."

" She wants you to ask leave always."

" I never used to do that," said Matilda. Her voice choked before she could finish her sentence.

" You will get into trouble."

" One trouble is better than another, though," said Matilda; and she went.

She went first to Mr. Sample's, and asked how much a pound of tea cost.

" The last I sent your aunt," said Mr. Sample, " was one fifty a pound; and worth it. Don't she approve the flavour?"

" I believe so. But I want a little of another kind, Mr. Sample — if you have any that is good, and not so high."

" I have an excellent Oolong here for a dollar. Will you try that?"

" Please give me a quarter of a pound."

" She will like it," said Mr. Sample, weighing the quantity and putting it up; " it really has as much body as the other sort, and I think it is very nearly as good. The other is fifty cents a pound more. Tell Mrs. Candy, I can serve her with this if she prefers."

"I want a loaf of bread too, if you please."

"Baking ,failed ?" said Mr. Sample. "Here Jem, give this little girl a loaf."

. He himself went to attend another custo-mer, so Matilda paid for her purchases without any more questions being asked her. She went to another store for a little butter, and there also laid in a few herrings; and then with a full basket and a light heart took the way to Lilac lane.

CHAPTER III.

MRS. ELDRIDGE was as she had left her yesterday; a trifle more forlorn, perhaps. The afternoon being bright and sunny, made everything in the house look more grimy and dusty for the contrast. Matilda shrank from having anything to do with it. But yet, the consciousness that she carried a basket of comfort on her arm was a great help.

"Good morning, Mrs. Eldridge; how do you do?" she said cheerily.

"Is it that little gal?"

"Yes, it is I, Mrs. Eldridge. I said I would come back. How do you do, to-day?"

"I'm most dead," said the poor woman. Matilda was startled; but looking again, could not see that her face threatened anything like it. She rather thought Mrs. Eldridge was tired of life; and she did not wonder.

" You don't feel sick, do you?"

" No" — the woman said with a long drawn sigh. "There ain't no sickness got hold o' me yet. There's no one as 'll care when it comes."

" Would you like a cup of tea this afternoon?"

" Tea?" said the poor woman, "I don't have no tea, child. Tea's for the folks as has money; or somebody to care for 'em."

" But I care for you," said Matilda gently. "And the Lord Jesus cares. And he gave me the money to get some tea, and I've got it. Now I'm going to make a fire in the stove. Is there any wood anywhere?"

" Fire?" said Mrs. Eldridge.

" Yes. To boil the kettle, you know. Is there any wood anywhere?"

" Have you got some tea?"

" Yes, and now I want to make the kettle boil. Where can I get some wood ? "

" Kettle ? " said the old woman. "I hain't no kettle."

" No tea-kettle ? "

" No. It's gone. There ain't none."

" What is there then, that I can boil some water in ? "

" There's a skillet down in there," said Mrs. Eldridge, pointing to the under part of the corner cupboard which Matilda had looked into the day before. She went now to explore what remained. The lower part had once been used, it seemed, for pots and kettles and stove furniture. At least it looked black enough; and an old saucepan and a frying pan, two flat-irons very rusty, and a few other iron articles were there. But both saucepan and frying pan were in such a state that Matilda could not think of using them. Days of purification would be needed first. So she shut the cupboard door, and came back to the question of fire; for difficulties were not going to overcome her now. And there were difficulties. Mrs. Eldridge could not help her to any firing. She knew nothing about it. None had been in the house for a long time.

Matilda stood and looked at the stove. Then she emptied her basket; laying her little packages carefully on a chair; and went off on a foraging expedition. At a lumber yard or a carpenter's shop she could pick- up something; but neither was near. The houses in Lilac lane were too needy themselves to ask anything at them. Matilda went down the lane, seeing no prospect of help, till she came to the iron shop and the livery stable. She looked hard at both places. Nothing for her purpose was to be seen; and she remembered that there were children enough in the houses behind her to keep the neighbourhood picked clean of chips and brushwood. What was to be done? She took a bold resolve, and went into the iron shop, the master of which she knew slightly.

He was there, and looked at her as she came in.

"Mr. Swain, have you any little bits of wood that you could let me have? bits of wood to make a fire."

"Matilda Englefield, ain't it?" said Mr. Swain. "Bits o' wood? bits of iron are more in our way — could let ye have a heap o' *them* — Bits o' wood to make a fire, did ye say? 'twon't be a big fire as 'll come out o' that 'ere little basket."

"I do not want a big fire — just some bits of wood to boil a kettle."

"I want to know!" said Mr. Swain. "You hain't come all this way from your house to get wood? What's happened to you?"

"O not for *our* fire! O no. I want it for a place here in the lane."

"These folks picks up their own wood — you hadn't no need for to trouble yourself about them."

"No, but it is some one who cannot pick up her own wood, Mr. Swain, nor get it any other way; it is an old woman, and she wants a little fire to make a cup of tea."

" I guess, if she can get the tea she can get the wood."

" Somebody brought her the tea," said Matilda, who luckily was not in one way a timid child. " I will pay for the wood if I can get some."

" O, that's the game, eh ?" said the man. " Well, as it's Mis' Englefield's daughter — I guess we'll find you what will do you — how 'll this suit, if I split it up for you, eh ? "

He handled an old box cover as he spoke.

Matilda answered that it was the very thing; and a few easy blows of Mr. Swain's hatchet broke it up into nice billets and splin- ters. Part of these went into Matilda's basket, one end of them at least; the rest she took with great difficulty in her apron; and so went back up the lane again.

It was good to see the glint of the old woman's eyes, when she saw the wood flung down on the floor. Matilda went on to clear

out the stove.   It had bits of coal and clinker
in the bottom of it.   But she had furnished
herself with a pair of old gloves, and her spirit
was thoroughly up to the work now.   She
picked out the coal and rubbish, laid in paper
and splinters and wood; now how to kindle
it?   Matilda had no match.   And she remembered suddenly that she had better have
her kettle ready first, lest the fire should burn
out before its work was done.   So saying to
Mrs. Eldridge that she was going after a
match, she went forth again.   Where to ask?
One house looked as forbidding as another.
Finally concluded to try the first.

She knocked timidly and went in.   A
slatternly woman was giving supper to a half
dozen children who were making a great deal
of noise over it.   The hurly burly confused
Matilda, and confused the poor woman
too.

"What do you want?" she asked shortly.

"I came to see if you could lend me a
tea-kettle for half an hour."

" What do you.want of my tea-kettle ? "

" I want only to boil some water."

" Hush your noise, Sam Darcy ! " said the woman to an urchin some ten years old who was clamouring for the potatoes, — " Who for ? "

" To boil some water for Mrs. Eldridge."

" You don't live here ? "

" No."

" Well, my tea-kettle's in use, you see. The cheapest way 'd. be for Mrs. Eldridge to get a tea-kettle for herself. Sam Darcy ! if you lay a finger on them 'taters till I give 'em to you " —

Matilda closed the door and went over the way. Here she found a somewhat tidy woman at work ironing. Nobody else in the room. She made known her errand. The woman looked at her doubtfully.

" If I let you take my kettle, I don't know when I'll see it agin. Mis' Eldridge don't have the use of herself so 's she kin come over the street to bring it back, ye see."

"I will bring it back myself," said Matilda. "I only want it for a little while."

"Is Mis' Eldridge sick?"

"No. I only want to make her a cup of tea."

"I hadn't heerd nothin' of her bein' sick. Be you a friend o' hern?"

". Yes."

"We've got sickness in *this* house," the woman went on. "And everythin's wantin' where there's sickness; and hard to get it. It's my old mother. She lies in there," (nodding towards an inner room) "night and day and day and night; and she'd like a bit o' comfort now and then as well as another; and 'tain't often as I kin give it to her. Life's hard, to them as hain't got nothin' to live on. I hadn't ought to complain, and I don't complain; but sometimes it comes over me that Life's hard."

Here was another!

"What does she want?" Matilda asked. "Is she very sick?"

" She won't never be no better," her daughter answered; " and she lies there and knows she won't never be no better; and she's all as full of aches as she kin be, sometimes; and other times she's more easy like; but she lies there and knows she can't never get up no more in this world; and she wants 'most everythin'. I do what I kin."

" Do you think you can lend me your tea-kettle? I will be very much obliged."

" Well, if you'll bring it back yourself, — I 'spose I will. It's all the kettle I've got."

She fetched it out of a receptacle behind the stove, brushed the soot from its sides with a chicken's wing, and handed it to Matilda. It was an iron tea-kettle, not very large to be sure, but very heavy to hold at arm's length; and so Matilda was obliged to carry it, for fear of smutching her frock. She begged a match too, and hastened back over the street as well as she could. But Matilda's heart, though glad at the comfort she was about to give, began to be wearily heavy on account of the comfort she could not give; comfort that was lacking in so many quarters where she could do nothing. She easily kindled her fire now; filled the tea-kettle at the pump, (this was very difficult, but without more borrowing she could not help it) and at last got the kettle on and had the joy of hearing it begin to sing. The worst came now. For that teacup and saucer and plate must be washed before they could be used; and Matilda could not bear to touch them. She thought of taking the unused cup at the back of the shelf. But conscience would not let her. " You know those ought to be washed," said conscience; "and if you do not do it, perhaps nobody else will." Matilda earnestly wished that somebody else might. She had no bowl, either, to wash them in, and no napkin to dry them. And here a dreadful thought suggested itself. Did Mrs. Eldridge herself, too, do without washing? There were no towels to be seen anywhere. Sick at heart, the little girl gathered up the soiled pieces of crockery in her basket (the basket had a paper in it) and went over the way again to Mrs. Rogers' cottage. As she went, it crossed her mind, could Mrs. Rogers perhaps be the other one of those two in Lilac lane who needed to have the Bible read to them? Or were there still others! And how many Christians there had need to be in the world, to do all the work of it. Even in Shadywalk. And what earnest Christians they had need to be.

"Back again a'ready?" said the woman, as she let her in. Matilda shewed what she had in her basket, and asked for something to wash her dishes in. She got more than she asked for; Sabrina Rogers took them from her to wash them herself.

"She has nobody to do any thing for her," Matilda observed of the poor old owner of the cup and saucer.

"She ain't able to do for herself," remarked Sabrina; "that's where the difference is. The folks as has somebody to do su'thin' for them, is lucky folks. I never see none o' that luck myself."

" But your mother has you," said Matilda gently.

" I can't do much for her, either," said Sabrina. " Poor folks must take life as they find it. And they find it hard."

" Can your mother read ? "

" She's enough to do to lie still and bear it, without readin'," said the daughter. " Folks as has to get their livin', has to do without readin'."

" But would she like it ? " Matilda asked.

" I wonder when these things *was* washed afore," said the woman, scrubbing at them. " Like it ? You kin go in and ask her."

Matilda pushed open the inner door and somewhat reluctantly went in. It was decent, that room was ; and this disabled old woman lay under a patchwork quilt, on a bed that seemed comfortable. But the window was shut and the air was close. It was very disa- greeable.

"How do you do to-day, Mrs. Rogers?" Matilda said, stepping nearer the bed.

"Who's that?" was the question.

"Matilda Englefield."

"Who's 'Tilda Eggleford?"

"I live in the village," said Matilda. "Are you much sick?"

"Laws, I be!" said the poor woman. "It's like as if my bones was on fire, some nights. Yes, I be sick. And I'll never be no better."

"Does anybody ever come to read the Bible to you?"

"Read the Bible?" the sick woman repeated. Her face looked dull, as if there had ceased to be any thoughts behind it. Matilda wondered if it was because she had so little to think of. "What about reading the Bible?" she said.

"You cannot read, lying there, can you?"

"There ain't a book nowheres in the house."

"Not a Bible?"

"A Bible? I hain't seen a Bible in five year."

"Do you remember what is in the Bible?" said Matilda, greatly shocked. This *was* living without air.

"Remember?" said the woman. "I'm tired o' 'membering. I'd like to go to sleep and remember no more. What's the use?"

"What do you remember?" Matilda asked in some awe.

"I remember 'most everything," said the woman wearily. "Times when I was well and strong — and young — and had my house comfor'ble and my things respectable. Them times was once. And I had what I wanted, and could do what I had a mind to. There ain't no use in remembering. I'd like to forget. Now I lie here."

"Do you remember nothing else?" said Matilda.

"I remember it all," said the woman. "I've nothin' to do but think. When I was first married, and just come home, and thought all the world was" — she stopped to sigh — "a garden o' posies. 'Tain't much like it, — to poor folks. And I had my children around me — Sabriny's the last on 'em. She's out there, ain't she?"

" Yes."

" What's she doin'?"

" She is ironing."

" Yes; she takes in. Sabriny has it all to do. I can't do nothin' — this five year."

" May I come and see you again, Mrs. Rogers? I must go now."

" You may come if you like," was the answer. " I don't know what you should want to come for."

Matilda was afraid her fire of pine sticks would give out; and hurried across the lane again with her basket of clean things. The stove had fired up, to be sure; and Mrs. Eldridge was sitting crouched over it, with an evident sense of enjoyment that went to Matilda's heart. If the room now were but clean, she thought, and the other room; and

the bed made, and Mrs. Eldridge herself—
There was too much to think of; Matilda
gave it up, and attended to the business in
hand. The kettle boiled. She made the tea
in the teacup; laid a herring on the stove;
spread some bread and butter; and in a few
minutes invited Mrs. Eldridge's attention to
her supper spread on a chair. The old
woman drank the tea as if it were the rarest
of delicacies; Matilda filled up her cup again;
and then she fell to work on the fish and
bread and butter, tearing them to pieces with
her fingers, and in great though silent appre-
ciation. Meanwhile Matilda brought the
cupboard to a little order; and then filling
up Mrs. Eldridge's cup for the third time,
carried back the kettle to Sabrina Rogers
and begged the loan of an old broom.

"What do you want to do with it?"

"Mrs. Eldridge's room wants sweeping
very much."

"Likely it does! Who's a going to sweep
it, though, if I lend you my broom?"

" There's nobody but me," said Matilda.

The woman brought the broom and as she gave it, asked, " Who sent you to do all this ? "

" Nobody."

" What made you come, then ?　It's queer play for a child like you."

" Somebody must do it, you know," said Matilda ; and she ran away.

But Sabrina's words recurred to her. It was queer play. But then, who would do it ?　And it was not for Mrs. Eldridge alone. She brushed away with a good heart, while the poor old woman was hovering over the chair on which her supper was set, munching bread and herring with a particularity of attention which shewed how good a good meal was to her. Matilda did not disturb her, and she said never a word to Matilda ; till, just as the little girl had brought all the sweepings of the floor to the threshold, where they lay in a heap, and another stroke of the broom would have scattered them into the street, the space outside the door was darkened by a figure the sight of which nearly made the broom fly out of Matilda's hand. Nobody but Mr. Richmond stood there. The two faces looked mutual pleasure and surprise at each other.

" Mr. Richmond! "

" What *are* you doing here, Tilly? "

" Mr. Richmond, can you step over this muss?   I will have it away directly."

Mr. Richmond stepped in, looked at the figure by the stove, and then back at Matilda. The little girl finished her sweeping and came back, to receive a warm grasp of the hand from her minister; one of the things Matilda liked best to get.

" Is all this your work, Tilly? " he whispered.

" Mr. Richmond, nobody has given her a cup of tea in a long while."

The minister stepped softly to the figure still bending over the broken herring; I think his blue eye had an unusual softness in it.

The old woman pushed her chair back and looked up at him.

" It's the minister agin," said she.

" Are you glad to see me ? " said Mr. Richmond, taking a chair that Matilda had dusted for him ; I am afraid she took off her apron to do it with, but the occasion was pressing. There was no distinct answer to the minister's question.

" You seem to have had some supper here," he remarked.

" It's a good cup o' tea," said Mrs. Eldridge ; —" a good cup o' tea. I hain't seen such a good cup o' tea, not since ten year ! "

" I am very glad of that. And you feel better for it, don't you ? "

" A good cup o' tea — makes one feel like folks," Mrs. Eldridge assented.

" And it is pleasant to think that somebody cares for us," Mr. Richmond went on.

" I didn't think as there warn't nobody," said Mrs. Eldridge wiping her lips.

" You see you were mistaken. Here are two people that care for you."

"She cares the most," said Mrs. Eldridge, with a little nod of her head towards Matilda.

"I will not dispute that," said the minister laughing. "She has cared fire and tea and bread and fish, — hasn't she? and you think I have only cared to come and see you. Don't you like that?"

"I used fur to have visits," said the poor old woman, — "when I had a nice place, and was fixed up respectable. I had visits. Yes, I had. There don't no one come now. There won't no more on 'em come. No more."

"Perhaps you are mistaken, Mrs. Eldridge. Do you see how much you were mistaken in thinking that no one cared for you? Do you know there is more care for you than hers?"

"I don't know why she cares," said Mrs. Eldridge.

"Who do you think sent her, and told her to care for you?"

"Who sent her" — the woman repeated.

"Yes, who sent her. Who do you think it was?"

As he got but a lack-lustre look in reply, the minister went on.

" This little girl is the servant of the Lord Jesus Christ; and he sent her to come and see you and care for you; and he did that because *he* cares. He cares about you. He loves you, and sent his little servant to be his messenger."

" He didn't send no one afore," the old woman remarked.

" Yes, he did," said Mr. Richmond, growing grave, — " he sent others, but they did not come. They did not do what he gave them to do. And now, Mrs. Eldridge, we bring you a message from the Lord — this little girl and I do, — that he loves you and wants you to love him. You know you never have loved, or trusted, or obeyed him, in all your life. And now, the goodness of God leadeth thee to repentance."

" 'There ain't much as a poor old thing like I can do," she said after a long pause.

" You can trust the Lord that died for you,

and love him, and thank him.   You can give
yourself to the Lord Jesus, to be made pure
and good. Can't you?   Then he will fit you
for his glorious place up yonder.   You must be
fitted for it, you know.   Nothing that defileth
or is defiled can go in; only those that have
washed their robes and made them white in
the blood of the Lamb.   Listen now while
I read about that."

Mr. Richmond opened his Bible and read,
first the seventh chapter of the Revelation and
then the twenty-second; and Matilda, standing and leaning on the back of his chair,
thought how wonderful the words were; that
even so poor an old helpless creature as the
one opposite him might come to have a share
in them.   Perhaps the wonder and the beauty
of them struck Mrs. Eldridge too; for she
listened very silently.   And then Mr. Richmond knelt down and prayed.

After that, he and Matilda together took
the way home.   The evening was falling;
and soft and sweet the light and the air came

through the trees, and breathed even over
Lilac lane. The minister and the little girl
together drew fresh breaths. It was all so
delicious after the inside of the poor house
where they had been.

"Light is a pleasant thing!" said the
minister, half to himself. "I think, Matilda,
heaven will seem something so, when we get
there."

"Like this evening, Mr. Richmond?"

"Like this evening light and beauty, after
coming out of Mrs. Eldridge's house."

"And then, will this world seem like Mrs.
Eldridge's house?"

"I think it will,—in the contrast. Look
at those dainty little flecks of cloud yonder,
low down in the sky, that seem to have
caught the light in their vaporous drapery
and embodied it. See what brilliance of
colour is there, and upon what a pure sky
beyond!"

"Will *this* ever seem like Mrs. Eldridge's
house?" said Matilda.

"This is the world that God made," said the minister smiling. "I was thinking of the world that man has made."

"Lilac lane, Mr. Richmond?" said Matilda glancing around her. They were hardly out of it.

"Lilac lane is not such a bad specimen," said the minister, with a sigh this time. "There is much worse than this, Matilda. And the worst of Lilac lane is what you do not see. — You had to buy your opportunity, then?" he added with a smile again, looking down at Matilda.

"I suppose I had, Mr. Richmond."

"What did you pay?"

"Mr. Richmond, it was not pleasant to think of touching Mrs. Eldridge's things."

"No. I should think not. But you are not sorry you came? Don't you find, that as I said, it pays?"

"O yes, sir! But" —

"But what?"

"There is so much to do."

" Yes ! " — said the minister thoughtfully. And it seemed to have stopped his talk.

" Is Mrs. Rogers the other one ? " Matilda asked.

" The other one ? " repeated Mr. Richmond.

" The other opportunity. You said there were two in Lilac lane, sir."

" I do not know Mrs. Rogers."

" But she is another one that wants the Bible read to her, Mr. Richmond. She lives just across the way — I found her out by going to borrow a tea-kettle."

" You borrowed your tea-kettle ? "

" Yes, sir. Mrs. Eldridge has none. She has almost nothing, and as she says, there is nobody that cares."

" Well, that will not do," said the minister. " We must see about getting a kettle for her."

" Then, Mr. Richmond, Mrs. Rogers is a *third* opportunity. She has been sick abed for five years, and there is not a Bible in the house."

"There are opportunities starting up on every side, as soon as we are ready for them," said the minister.

"But Mr. Richmond — I am afraid, — I am not ready for them."

"Why so, my dear child? I thought you *were.*"

"I am afraid I was sorry when I found out about Mrs. Rogers."

"Why were you sorry?"

"There seemed so much to do, Mr. Richmond! so much disagreeable work. Why, it would take every bit of time I have got, — and more, — to attend to those two; every bit."

There came a rush of something that for a moment dimmed Mr. Richmond's blue eyes; and for a moment he was silent. And for that moment too the language of gold clouds and sky was a sharp answer — the answer of Light, — to the thoughts of earth.

"It is very natural," — Mr. Richmond said. "It is a natural feeling."

"But it is not right, is it?" said Matilda timidly.

"Is it like Jesus?"

"No, sir."

"Then it cannot be right. 'Who being in the form of God, thought it not robbery to be equal with God: but made himself of no reputation, and took upon himself the form of a servant, and was made in the likeness of men: and being found in fashion as a man, he humbled himself and became obedient unto death, even the death of the cross.'

"Who 'pleased not himself.' Who 'had not where to lay his head.' Who, 'though he was rich, yet for our sakes he became poor.' 'He laid down his life for us; and we ought to lay our lives down for the brethren.'"

Matilda listened, with a choking feeling coming in her throat.

"But then, what can I do, Mr. Richmond? how can I help feeling so?"

"There is only one way, dear Matilda,"

said her friend. " The way is, to love Jesus so much, that you like his will better than your own; so much, that you would rather please him than please yourself."

" How can I get that, Mr. Richmond ? "

" Where we get all other good things. Ask the Lord to reveal himself in your heart, so that the love of him may take full possession."

The walk was silent for the greater part of the remaining way; silent and pleasant. The colours of sunset faded away, but a cool, fair, clear heaven carried on the beauty and the wordless speech of the earlier evening. At Matilda's gate Mr. Richmond stopped, and holding her hand still, spoke with a bright smile.

" I will give you a text to think about and pray over, Matilda."

" Yes, Mr. Richmond."

" Keep it, and think of it, and pray about it, till you understand it, and love it."

" Yes, Mr. Richmond. I will."

" The words are these. You will find them in the fourth chapter of the second epistle to the Corinthians."

" In the fourth chapter of the second epistle to the Corinthians. Yes, sir."

" These are the words. ' Always bearing about in the body the dying of the Lord Jesus, that the life also of Jesus might be made manifest in our body.' Good night."

CHAPTER IV.

MATILDA thought so much over Lilac lane and the words Mr. Richmond had given her, that Maria charged her with being unsociable. Much Matilda wished that she could have talked with her sister about those same words; but Maria was in another line.

"You are getting so wrapped up in yourself," she said, "there is no comfort in you. I might as well have no sister. And I guess aunt Candy means I sha'n't. She gives you all the good times, up in her room, among the pretty things; I am only fit for washing dishes. Well, it's her opinion. It isn't mine."

"I don't have a good time up there, Maria, indeed. I would a great deal rather be down here washing dishes, or doing any thing."

"What do you go there for, then?"

"I have to go."

"We didn't use to *have to* do anything, when mamma was living. I wouldn't do it if I were you, if I didn't like it."

"I don't like it," said Matilda; "but I think I ought to do what aunt Candy wishes, as long as it is not something wrong."

"She'll come to that," said Maria; "or it'll be something you will think wrong; and then we shall have a time! I declare, I believe I shall be glad!"

"What for, Maria?"

"Why! Then I shall have you again. You'll come on my side. It's lonely, to have the dirty work all to myself. I don't suppose *you* mind it."

"Indeed but I do," said Matilda. "I don't like to sit upstairs darning stockings."

"And reading. And I don't know what."

"The reading is worse," said Matilda sighing. "It is something I do not understand."

"What does she make you do it for?"

"I don't know," said Matilda with another sigh. "But I want to do something else dreadfully, all the time."

The darning was very tedious indeed the morning after this talk. Matilda had got her head full of schemes and plans that looked pleasant; and she was eager to turn her visions into reality. It was stupid to sit in her aunt's room, taking up threads on her long needle exactly and patiently, row after row. It had to be done exactly, or Mrs. Candy would have made her pick it all out again.

"Yes, that is very well; that is neat," said Mrs. Candy, when Matilda brought her the stocking she had been at work on, with the heel smoothly run. "That will do. Now you may begin. upon another one. There they are, in that basket."

"But aunt Candy," said Matilda in dismay, "don't you think I have learned now how to do it?"

"Yes, pretty well."

" Then, need I do any more?"

" A little further practice will not hurt you. Practice makes perfect, you know."

" But do you mean that I must darn all those stockings."

" Aren't they yours?"

" Yes, ma'am—I believe they are."

" Who should darn them then?"

Matilda very sorrowfully remembered the hand which did darn them once and thought it no hardship. Her hand went swiftly up to her eyes before she spoke again.

" I think it is right I should do them; and I will. May I take them away and do them in my own room?"

" You may do exactly what I tell you, my dear."

" Does it make any difference, aunt Candy?"

" That is something you need not consider. All you have to do is to obey orders. The more promptly and quietly, the easier for you, Matilda."

Matilda coloured, bridled, kept down the wish to cry, and began upon the second heel of her stockings. She was tired of that long needle and its long needleful of double thread.

"Matilda," said her aunt, "put down your stocking and look at me."

Which Matilda did, much surprised.

"When you wish to answer any thing I say, I prefer always that you should answer me in words."

"Ma'am?" said Matilda.

"You heard me."

"But I did not understand you."

"Again!" said Clarissa.

"I do not like to be answered by gestures. Do you understand that?"

"No, ma'am; I do not know what you mean by saying it."

"You do not know that you answered me by a toss of your head just now?"

"No, ma'am; certainly not."

"I am very glad to hear it. Don't do it again."

It would have been very like Matilda to do it again just there; but bewilderment quite put down other emotions for the time. Except the sense of being wronged; and that is a feeling very hard to bear. Matilda had scarcely known it before in her little life; the sensation was as new as it was painful. She was utterly unconscious of having done anything that ought to be found fault with. The darning needle went very fast for the next half hour; and Matilda's cheek was bright.

"They haven't got a fire upstairs, have they?" Maria questioned, when her little sister rejoined her.

"No, not to-day. Why?"

"You look as if you had been somewhere where it was warm."

But Matilda did not say what sort of fire had warmed her.

She forgot all about it and about all other grievances, as soon as she was free to go out in the afternoon. For now some of her visions were to be realized. Yesterday afternoon had been so pleasant, on the whole, that Matilda determined to seek a renewal of the pleasure. And first and foremost, she had determined to get Mrs. Eldridge a tea-kettle. She had money enough yet; only her Bible and yesterday's purchases had come out of her twenty-five dollars. "A tea-kettle — and what else?" thought Matilda. "Some towels? She does dreadfully want some towels. But then, I cannot get everything!"

Slowly going towards the corner, with her eyes on the ground, her two hands were suddenly seized by somebody and she was brought to a stand-still.

"Norton!" cried Matilda joyously.

"Yes. What has become of you?"

"O I have been so busy!"

"School?" said Norton.

"O no; I don't go to school. I have things to do at home."

"Things!" said Norton. "Why don't you speak straight? What things? your lessons?"

"I don't have lessons, Norton," said the child patiently, lifting her eyes to Norton's face. "My aunt gives me other things.to do."

"Don't you have lessons at all?" said Norton.

"Not now. I wish I did."

"Where are you going now, Pink?"

"Pink!" echoed Matilda.

"Yes, that's your name. Where are you going? Come home with me."

"I have got business, Norton."

"You haven't got" — said Norton peering round — "Yes, I declare she *has* got — that Bible tucked under her arm! Are you going to see nobody again?"

Matilda nodded.

"I'll go too," said Norton, "and find out what it all means. Give. me the book, and I'll carry it."

"But Norton!" said Matilda holding the Bible fast, "I would like to have you, but I am afraid you wouldn't like it."

"Like what, Pink? The Bible?"

"O no.   O *yes*, I wish you did like that; but I mean, where I am going."

"Do you like it?"

"I like to go.   I don't like the place, Norton, for the place is very disagreeable."

"So I should think.   But I might like to go too, you know.   I'm going to try."

Matilda stood still and looked very dubious.

"I'm going," Norton repeated laughing. "You want me to go, don't you?"

"Why I would like it very much, if you would not"—

"What?   No, I will not," said Norton shaking his head.

"But Norton, I am going into Mr. Forshew's, first."

"Well; I can go into Mr. Forshew's too. I've been *there* before."

"I am going to buy a tea-kettle."

"I shall not interfere with that," said Norton.

"But I am going to get a tea-kettle and take it along with me; to Lilac lane."

" What for ? They'll send it if you want it."

" I want it immediately; and Mr. Forshew's boy is never there when he is wanted, you know."

" *You* want the tea-kettle immediately. You are not going to make tea immediately, are you ? "

" Exactly that, Norton. That is one of the things I am going to do. And the poor old woman I am going to see, has no tea-kettle."

" Then I don't believe she has tea."

" O yes, but I know she has tea, Norton."

" And bread and butter ? "

" Yes, and bread and butter too," said Matilda, nodding her little head positively. Norton looked at her with a perfectly grave face.

" It must be a very odd house," said he, " I don't see how you can be so sure of things."

Matilda began to walk on towards the corner.

" Who took her tea and bread and butter ? "

said Norton. "I suppose you know, if you know the rest."

" Of course, somebody must have done it," said Matilda hesitating.

" I wonder if there was a Pink anywhere among the things," said Norton. "Did you see anything of it?"

Matilda could not help laughing, and they both laughed; and so they went into Mr. Forshew's shop. It was a little low shop, just on the corner; but to be sure, there was a great variety and a good collection of things there. All sorts of iron things, and a great many sorts of tin things; with iron dust and street dust plentifully overlying the shop and everything in it. Stoves were there in variety; chains and brooms and coalskuttles; coffee-mills and axes and lamps; tin pails and earthen batter jars; screws and nails and hinges and locks; and a telegraph operator was at work in a corner. Several customers were there too; Matilda had to wait.

" It is odd now," said Norton. " I suppose,

if I wanted to spend money here, I should buy everything else in the world *but* a tea-kettle. That's what it is to be a girl."

" Nonsense!" said Matilda, and the set of her head was inimitable.   Norton laughed.

" That's what it is to be a Pink," he said. "I forgot.   I don't believe there is another girl in town wants a tea-kettle but you. What else do you want, Pink?"

" A great deal," said Matilda; " but I can't get all I want."

" You don't want an axe, for instance; nor a coffee-mill; nor a tin pail, nor an iron chain, nor a dipper; nor screws, nor tacks; nor a lamp, do you? nor a box of matches" —

"O yes, Norton! O yes, that is just what I do want; a box of matches.   I never should have thought of it."

" How about stoves, Pink?   Here are plenty."

" She has a stove.   Don't be ridiculous, Norton."

And Mr. Forshew being just then at leisure, Matilda purchased a little tin tea-kettle and came out with it in triumph.

"Now is that all?" said Norton. "How about the bread and butter? Perhaps it has given out."

"No, I think not. I guess there is enough. Perhaps we had better take another loaf of bread, though. We shall pass the baker's on our way."

"Have you got money enough for everything you want, Pink? does your aunt give you whatever you ask for?"

"O I never ask her for anything," said Matilda.

"Take it without asking?"

"I do not ask, and she does not give me, Norton. But once she did, when she first came; she gave me, each of us, twenty-five dollars. I have got that, all that is left of it."

"How much is left of it?"

"Why, I don't know exactly. I spent four dollars for something else; then eighty-five cents yesterday, and a dollar just, to-day. That makes " —

" Five eighty-five," said Norton. "And that out of twenty-five, leaves nineteen fifteen."

" I've got that, then," said Matilda.

" And no hope of more ? That won't do, Pink. Nineteen dollars won't last for ever at this rate. Here's the baker's."

The bread Norton paid for and carried off; and the two stepped along briskly to Lilac lane.

Matilda was very glad privately that she had swept Mrs. Eldridge's floor yesterday. The place looked so much the more decent; though as it was, Norton cast his eyes around him whistling low, and Matilda knew well enough that he regarded it as a very odd place for either himself or Pink to find themselves in.

" What's to be done now ? " he inquired of her, as she was putting the bread and matches on a shelf of the cupboard.

" The first thing is to make a fire, Norton.

I've got wood enough here. And the matches."

"*You* have got" — said Norton stooping to fetch out the sticks from the lower cupboard where Matilda had stowed them. "Did you get it? Where did you get it?"

"Mr. Swain split it up for me, — at the iron shop, you know."

"Did you go to the iron shop for it? And bring it back yourself?"

"There was nobody else to do it," said Matilda.

"You're a brick!" said Norton. "That's what I said. But is this all, Pink?"

"It is plenty, Norton."

"Plenty for to-day. It won't last for any more. What then?"

"I don't know," said Matilda. " O Norton, are *you* going to make the fire?"

Norton shewed that such was his intention, and shewed besides that he knew very well what he was about. Matilda, after looking on admiringly, ran off to the pump with her kettle. The pump was at some distance; before she could fill her kettle and come back, Norton overtook her. He quietly assumed the tea-kettle as a matter of course.

"O thank you, Norton! how good you are," Matilda exclaimed. "It was heavy."

"Look here. Do you come here to do this sort of thing all by yourself?" said Norton.

"I cannot help that," said Matilda. "And I like to do it, too."

"You mustn't"—said Norton.

"Who will, then, Norton? And the poor old woman cannot do anything for herself."

"Isn't there somebody in the world to take care of her?"

"No; nobody."

"That's a shame. And I don't believe it, either."

"O but there is nobody, Norton. She is quite alone. And if some one will not help her, she must go without everything."

Norton said no more, but he looked very much disgusted with this state of society.

He silently watched what Matilda was doing, without putting in any hinderance or hinting at any annoyance further; which she thought was very good of him. Instead of that, he looked after the fire and lifted the kettle when it was needful. Matilda as yesterday made the tea and spread bread and butter and cooked a herring; and then had the satisfaction of seeing the poor old woman luxuriating over what was to her a delicious meal. She had said very little since their coming in; but eyed all they did, with a gradual relaxing of the lines of her face. Something like pleasure, something like comfort, was stealing into her heart and working to soften those hard lines. Matilda waited now until the meal should be quite finished before she brought forward anything of different interest.

"That's a new kettle," — was the first remark, made while Matilda was clearing away the remains of the supper.

"How do you like it?" said Norton.

The old woman looked at him, she had done that a great deal already, and answered, " Who be you ? "

" I'm the fellow that brought the kettle from the shop," said Norton.

" Whose kettle is it ? "

" It ought to be your's — it's on your stove."

" It is your's, Mrs. Eldridge," said Matilda.

" Well, I hain't had a tea-kettle," said the old woman meditatively, " not since — I declare, I don't know when 'twas. I hain't had a tea-kettle, not since my old un fell down the well. I never could get it out. That one hadn't no kiver."

" Don't let this one get down in the well," said Norton.

" I shan't go to the well no more," said Mrs. Eldridge. " When I had a place, and a well, and a bucket, — it was good times ! That ain't my kettle."

" Yes, Mrs. Eldridge, it is," said Matilda. " It is your's ; and it just fits the stove hole."

"A kettle's a good thing," said the old woman. "It looks good."

"Now would you like to have a little reading again?" Matilda inquired, bringing out her Bible.

"Have you got anything more about the — what was it? I don' know what 'twas."

"About the shepherd? the Good Shepherd?"

"You may read a bit about that," said the old woman. "There ain't no shepherds now, is there?"

"Plenty of 'em," said Norton.

"It don't seem as if there was no place for 'em to keep the sheep. *I* don't see none. But he used for to be a shepherd; and he took good care of 'em, he did."

"The Lord Jesus is the Good Shepherd; and he takes good care of his sheep," said Matilda. "He cares for them always. He cares for you, Mrs. Eldridge."

The old woman made no answer to this; but instead, sat with so meditative a look upon her face that Matilda, though she had her book open to read, forbore, and waited.

-"Did he send you?" said Mrs. Eldridge.

Norton glanced a quick look of amusement at Matilda, but Matilda simply answered, "Yes."

"I didn't know as there was any one as cared," she said slowly.

Matilda began to read, upon that; giving her the twenty-third psalm again; then the tenth chapter of John; finishing with one or two passages in the Revelation. Norton stood in the doorway while she read, looking out and looking in, very quiet; and Mrs. Eldridge sat and listened and gave tremulous shakes of her old head, and was very quiet too.

"I must go now," said Matilda, when she had done and had paused a few minutes.

"It has a good sound"— said the old woman.

"It's true"— said Matilda.

And she and Norton took their leave. Then began a joyous walk home.

"Pink," said Norton, when they were got a little way from the house, — " you made your tea in a tea-cup."

" Yes; there is only a wretched little tin tea-pot there, not fit to be used; it is in such · a state."

" No spoons either? "

" No, and no spoons. There is hardly any thing there at all, Norton."

" I don't see how people come to be so poor," said Norton.

"No, *I* don't," said Matilda. " But she is old, you see, and cannot help herself, and has no one left that does care about her. Nobody in the world, I mean."

" That house is in a tremendous condition," said Norton. " For dirt I mean."

" Yes, I know it."

" I don't see why somebody hasn't cleaned it before now."

" Why Norton, who should do it? None of the neighbours care anything about her."

" Is she bad ? "

" No, Norton! not bad at all; but they are poor too, and sick, some of them; and they have their own work to do, and their own things to get, and they haven't anything to spare for her."

" She was glad of that tea-kettle."

"Wasn't she! I could see that."

" But I say, Pink! I don't see how people come to be so poor. There's money enough."

" For some people "— said Matilda.

" Money enough for everybody."

" Perhaps, — if it was divided "— said Matilda. " But Norton, it isn't. The rich people have got it almost all."

" Have they?" said Norton. " Then they ought to look out for such poor chaps as this."

" So I think, Norton," said Matilda eagerly.

" But Pink, *you* can't do it. You are only one, and you can't take care of all Lilac lane, to begin with. That's what I am thinking about."

" No, not all the lane. But 1 can do something. I can read to Mrs. Eldridge, and Mrs. Rogers.”

“You can’t buy tea-kettles, though, for Mrs. Eldridge and Mrs. Rogers, with the tea and the sugar and the bread and butter and the fish and the mutton chops they will all . want. Your nineteen dollars will soon be gone at that rate.”

“Mutton chops!” echoed Matilda. “Norton, they do not see anything so good as mutton chops.”

“They ought to,” said Norton. “They have as much right as other folks.”

“But they *can’t*, Norton.”

“Yes, they can, Pink. We’ll take ’em some for once. They shall know how mutton tastes.”

“Oh Norton!” said Matilda in a low voice of delight, “how good that would be!”

“But what I *say*,” continued the boy with emphasis, — “you cannot go on doing this. *Your* money will not last.”

“I can do what I can,” said Matilda softly.

" But what's the use, Pink? All you can do will just touch one old woman, perhaps, a few times; and then Lilac lane will not be any better off than it was. And anyhow, you only touch one. What's the use?"

" Why — the use of that one."

" Yes, but it don't really make any difference to speak of, when you think of all the people that you cannot help. The world won't be any better — don't you see?"

"If I was the one to be helped, I should think it made a great deal of difference, Norton."

Norton could not dispute that view of the case, though he whistled over it.

" Pink, will you come and play croquet to-morrow?"

" To-morrow? I will see if I can," said Matilda, with a brightening face.

" What's to hinder you?"

"I don't know that anything. If aunt Candy will let me."

" Does *she* hinder you?"

"Sometimes"— Matilda said hesitating.

"What for?"

"I do not know. That puzzles me, Norton."

"*How* does she hinder you?" said the boy stopping short with a scowl upon his brow.

"She won't let me go out, sometimes; I don't know why. Then besides, I have to spend a good deal of time reading to her, and darning stockings; and I have a great many other things to do, Norton."

"Well, come to-morrow, Pink; or I shall come after you. Hulloa! see that squirrel"—

And Norton set off on such a race and chase after the squirrel, that Matilda stopped to look on in sheer admiration. The race was not fruitful of anything however but admiration; and the rest of the way they hurried home.

It was a trembling question with Matilda, could she go to play croquet the next day? She could not go in her work dress; and she feared to change her dress and so draw attention, lest her aunt should put a stop to her going out át all. She debated the matter a good deal, and finally concluded to make an open affair of it and ask leave.

" To go to Mrs. Laval's," — said Mrs. Candy, meditating.

" Who is going to play croquet, besides you ? " inquired Clarissa.

" I do not think anybody is to be there besides me," said Matilda.

" Well " — said Mrs. Candy, " 1 suppose you had better go; with my compliments and thanks to Mrs. Laval. Put on your white dress, Matilda, and I will tie a ribband round your waist."

The white dress and the black ribband were duly put on, and Matilda set out; very happy indeed; only sorry that Maria was left behind. She got a glad welcome from Norton, who was at the iron gate watching for her. And when she came to the door of the house, Matilda was fain to stand still and look, everything was so beautiful. It was very different from last winter, when the snow covered all the world. Now the grass was soft and green, cut short and rolled smooth, and the sunlight made it seem almost golden. The rose bushes were heavy and sweet with great cabbage roses and delicate white roses, and gay-yellow roses made an elegant variety. Overhead the golden clusters of a laburnum tree dropped as if to meet them. Then there were pinks and violets and daisies; and locust trees a little way off, standing between the house and the sun, made the air sweet with their blossoms. Every breath was charged with some delicious perfume or other. The house stood hospitably and gayly open in summer dress; the farm country lay rich in the sun towards the west; and the mountains beyond, having lost all their white coating of snow long ago, were clothed in a kind of drapery of purple mist.

"What's the matter?" said Norton.

"It's so beautiful!" said Matilda.

"O is that all! Come in. Mamma wants to see you."

In the house, over floors marble and matted, through rooms green with the light that came through the blinds, cool in shadow, but from which the world without looked like a glittering fairyland, so they went, passing from one to another, till they found the mistress of the house. She was not in the house, but in a deep wicker chair on the shady side of the verandah.

"Here she is!" the lady exclaimed as she saw them, throwing aside the book which had been in her hands, and drawing Matilda into her arms instead. " My dear child — so you've come. Norton and I are very glad. How do you do? You are thin."

" Am I?" said Matilda.

"I am afraid you are. What are you going to do? play croquet? it's too warm yet. Sit down here and have some strawberries first. Norton, you get her some strawberries."

She put Matilda affectionately into a chair and took off her hat.

" And how do you like croquet?"

" O very much! But I do not know how to play yet," said Matilda.

" Norton will teach you."

" Yes, ma'am," Matilda said with a happy look.

" I think Norton is making a little sister of you," Mrs. Laval said tenderly, drawing her hand down Matilda's cheek. " Do you know, Norton once had a little sister as old as you ? "

The lady's tone had changed. Matilda only looked, she dared not speak in answer to this.

" I think he wants to make a sister of you," Mrs. Laval repeated wistfully, her hand dropping to Matilda's hand and taking hold of that. " How would you like to be Norton's sister ? "

" O I should like it very much!" Matilda answered, half eagerly, but her answer touched with a soberness that belonged to the little sister and daughter that Norton and Mrs. Laval had lost. There was a delicate, sensitive manner about both her face and her voice as she spoke, perfectly intelligible to the eyes that were watching her; and the response to it was startling. For Mrs. Laval suddenly took the child in her arms, upon her lap, though Matilda never knew how she got there, and clasping her close, half smothered her with kisses; some of which Matilda felt were wetted with tears. It was a passion of remembered tenderness and unsatisfied longing. Matilda was astonished and passive under caresses she could not return, so close was the clasp of the arms that held her, so earnest the pressure of the lips that seemed to devour every part of her face by turns. In the midst of this Norton came with the strawberries; and he too stood still and offered no interruption. But when a pause in Mrs. Laval's ecstasy gave him a chance, he said low,

" Mrs. Beechey, mamma, and Miss Beecheys, are there."

Mrs. Laval was quiet a moment, hiding her face in Matilda's neck; then she put her gently down, rose up, and met some ladies who were coming round the corner of the verandah, with a tone and bearing so cool and careless and light, that Matilda asked her ears if it was possible. The guests were carried off into the house; Matilda and Norton were left alone.

It was Matilda's turn then. She set down the plate of strawberries Norton had given her and hid her face in her hands.

Norton bore this for a minute, and no more. Then one of his hands came upon one of Matilda's, and the other upon the other, very gently but decidedly suggesting that they should come down.

" Pink!" said he, — "this may do for mamma and you, but it is very poor entertainment for me. Come! leave that, and eat your strawberries, and let us go on the lawn. The sun will do now."

Matilda felt that this was reasonable, and she put by her own gratification. Nevertheless her eyes and eyelashes were all glittering when she lifted them up.

"What has mamma done to you?" said Norton wondering. "Here, Pink, do you like strawberries?"

"If you please, Norton," said Matilda, "couldn't I have them another time? I don't want them now."

"Then they may wait till we have done playing," said Norton; "and then I'll have some too. Now come."

The great trees cast a flickering shadow on the grass before the house. Norton planted his hoops and distributed colours, and presently Matilda's sober thoughts were driven as many ways as the balls; and *they* went very widely indeed.

"You must take *aim*, Matilda?" Norton cried.

"At what?"

"Why you must learn at what; that's the

game.   You must fight.   Just as I fight you. You ought to touch my ball now, if you can. I don't believe you can.   You might try."

Matilda tried, and hit it.   The game went on prosperously.   The sun got lower, and the sunbeams came more scattering, and the breeze just stirred over the lawn; not enough to bend the little short blades of grass.   Mrs. Laval's visiters went away, and she came out on the verandah to look at the children; they were too much engaged to look at her.   At last the hard fought battle came to an end. Norton brought out another plate of strawberries for himself along with Matilda's, and the two sat down on the bank under the locust trees to eat them.   The sun was near going down beyond the mountains by this time, and his setting rays changed the purple mist into a bath of golden haze.

" How nice and cold these are," said Matilda.

" They have been in the ice.   That makes things cold," observed Norton.

" And being warm oneself makes them seem colder," said Matilda.

" Why, are you warm, Pink ? "

" Yes, indeed. I have had to fight you so hard, you know."

" You did very well," said Norton in a satisfied tone.

" Norton, how pretty it all is to-night."

Norton eat strawberries.

" Very different from Lilac lane," said Matilda looking at the china plate in her hand, on which the painting was very fine and delicate.

" Rather different," said Norton.

" Norton, — I was thinking of what you said yesterday ; how odd it is that some people should be rich and others poor."

" I am glad I am one of the first sort," said Norton, disposing of a very large strawberry.

" But isn't it strange ? "

" That is what I said, Pink."

" It don't seem right," said Matilda thought-fully

" Yes, it does."

" It doesn't to me."

" How can you help it ? "

" Why *I* cannot help it, Norton ; but if everybody that is rich chose, they could help it."

" How ? "

" Don't you think they ought ? "

" Well how, Pink ? If people were industrious and behaved right, they wouldn't be poor, you see."

" O but, Norton, they would sometimes. There is Mrs. Eldridge, and there are the poor women at Mrs. Rogers' ; and a great many more like them."

" Well if *somebody* hadn't behaved wrong," said Norton, " they wouldn't be so hard up."

" O but that does not help them."

" Not much."

" And they ought to be helped," said Matilda slowly, examining the painted flowers on the china in her hand, and remembering Mrs. Eldridge's cracked delf tea-cup.

" That plate would buy up the whole con-
cern where we were yesterday, wouldn't it? "

Matilda looked up suddenly, at Norton's
thus touching her thought; but she did not
like to pursue it.   Norton however had no
scruples.

" Yes; and these strawberries, I suppose,
would feed her for a week — the old woman,
I mean.   And one of our drawing room chairs
would furnish her house, pretty near.   Yes, I
guess it would.   And I really think one week
of the coal we burned a few months ago
would keep her, and Mrs. Rogers too, warm
all winter.   And I am certain one of mamma's dresses would clothe her for a year.
Seems queer, don't it."

" And *she* is cold and hungry and uncom-
fortable," said Matilda.   The two looked at
each other.

" But then, you know, if mamma gave one
of her dresses to clothe this old woman, she
would have to give another to clothe some
other old woman; and the end would be, she

would have no dresses for herself. And if she tried to warm all the cold houses, she wouldn't have firing to cook her own dinner. You see it has to be so, Pink; some rich and some poor. And suppose these strawberries had been changed into some poor somebody's dinner, I couldn't have had them to give to you. Do you see, Pink?"

"But O, Norton!"— Matilda began, and stopped. "These strawberries are very nice."

"But you would rather turn them into mutton chops and give them away?" said Norton. "I dare say you would! Wouldn't you?"

"Norton," said Matilda cautiously, "do you think anything I *could* have bought with that dollar would have given me so much pleasure as that tea-kettle yesterday?"

"It was a good investment," said Norton. "But it is right to eat strawberries, Pink. Where are you going to stop?"

"I'll take Mrs. Eldridge some strawberries," said Matilda smiling, "when they get plenty."

"Well, agreed," said Norton. "Let us take her some other things too. I've got money. Stop—let me put these plates in the house and fetch a piece of paper; — then we'll see what we'll take her."

Matilda sat while he was gone, looking at the golden mist on the mountains and dreaming.

"Now," said Norton, throwing himself on the turf beside her, with his piece of paper, and thrusting his hand deep down in his pocket to get at his pencil, "now let us see what we will do."

"Norton," said Matilda joyously, "this is better than croquet."

Norton looked up with those bright eyes of his, but his reply was to proceed to business.

"Now for it, Pink. What shall we do for the old lady? What does she want? Pooh! she wants everything; but what to begin with?"

"Strawberries, you said."

"Strawberries! Not at all. That's the

last thing. I mean we'll fix her up, Pink. Now what does she want, to be comfortable. It is only one old woman; but we shall feel better if she is comfortable. Or you will."

"But what do you mean, Norton? how much *can* we do?"

"Just as much as we've a mind to. I've got money, I tell you. Come; begin. What goes down first?"

"Why Norton," said Matilda in an ecstasy, "it is like a fairy story."

"What?"

"This, that we are doing. It is like a fairy story exactly."

"How is it like fairy stories?" said Norton. "*I* don't know."

"Did you never read fairy stories?"

"Never. What are they like?"

"Why some of them are just like this," said Matilda. "People are rich, and can do what they please; and they set out to get things together for a feast, or to prepare a palace for some princess; and first one nice thing is got, and then another, and then something else; until by and by you feel as if you had been at the feast, or seen the palace, or had done the shopping. I do."

" This isn't for a princess," said Norton.

. " No, nor a palace," said Matilda; " but it seems just as good."

" Go on, Pink; let us quit princesses and get to the real business. What do you want to get, first thing?"

" *First* thing," said Matilda, " I think would be to get somebody to clean the house. There are only two little rooms. It wouldn't be much. Don't you think so, Norton?"

" As we cannot build a palace, and have it new, I should say the old one had better be cleaned."

" Sabrina Rogers would do it, I dare say," Matilda went on; " and maybe that would be something good for her."

" Teach her to clean her own?" said Norton.

"Why no, Norton; her own is clean. I meant, maybe she would be glad of the pay."

"There's another princess, eh, that wants a palace?" said Norton. "If we could, we would new build Lilac lane, wouldn't we? But then, I should want to make over the people that live in it."

"So should I; and that is the hardest. But perhaps, don't you think the people *would* be different, if they had things different?"

"I'm certain I should be different, if I lived where they do," said Norton. "But go on, Pink; let us try it on — what's her name. We have only cleaned her house yet."

"The first thing, then, is a bedstead, Norton."

"A bedstead! What does she sleep on?"

"On the floor; with rags and straw, and I think a miserable make-believe of a bed. No sheets, no blankets, nor anything. It is dreadful."

"Rags and straw," said Norton. "Then a bedstead wants a bed on·it, Pink? and blankets or coverlets or something, and sheets, and all that."·

Matilda watched Norton's pencil as it noted the articles.

"Then she wants some towels, and a basin of some sort to wash in."

"Hm!" said Norton. "Herself, I hope?"

"Yes, I hope so. But she has nothing to make herself clean with."

"Then a stand and basin and towels; and a pitcher, Pink, I suppose, to hold water."

"Yes, a pitcher or jug or something. We want to get the cheapest things we can. And soap."

"Let's have plenty of that," said Norton, putting down soap. "Now then — what next?"

"A little wooden table, Norton? she has nothing but a chair to set her tea on."

"A table. And a carpet?"

"O no, Norton; that's not necessary. It is warm weather now. She does not want that. But she *does* want a pail for water. I have to take the tea-kettle to the pump."

Norton at this laughed, and rolled over on the grass in his amusement. Having thus refreshed himself, he came back to business.

"Has she got anything to go on her fire, except a tea-kettle?"

"Not much. A saucepan would be a very useful thing, and not cost much. I bought one the other day; so I know."

"What's a saucepan?" said Norton. "A pan to make sauce in?"

It was Matilda's turn to laugh. "Poor Mrs. Eldridge don't have many puddings, I guess, to make sauce for," she said.

"Well Pink, now we come, don't we, to the eating line. We must stock her up."

"Put down a broom first, Norton."

"A broom! Here goes."

"Yes, you can't think how much I have wanted a broom there. And a tea-pot. O yes, and a little milk pitcher, and sugar bowl. Can't we?"

"I should think we could," said Norton. "Tea-cups?"

"I guess not. She's got two; and three plates. Now, Norton — the eatables. What did you think of?"

"I suppose there isn't anything in the house," said Norton.

"Nothing at all — except what we took there."

"Then she wants everything."

"But — You see, Norton, she can't do anything herself; she couldn't use some things. There would be no use."

"No use in what?"

"Flour, for instance. She couldn't make bread."

"I don't know anything about flour," said Norton. "But she can use bread when she sees it, I will take my affidavit."

"O yes, bread, Norton. We will take her some bread; and a little butter. And sugar.

And tea. She has got some, but it won't
last long."

"And I said she should have a mutton
chop."

"I dare say she would like it."

"I wonder if a bushel of potatoes wouldn't
be the best thing of all."

"Potatoes would be excellent," said Matilda delightedly. "I suppose she would be
very glad of anything of that sort. Let's
take her some cheese, Norton."

"Cheese. And strawberries. And cake,
Pink."

"I am afraid we should be taking too much
at once. We had better leave the cake to
another time."

"There's something we forgot," said Norton. "Mr. What's-his-name will not split up
box covers for your fire every day; we must
send in a load of firing. Wood, I guess."

"O how good!" said Matilda. "You see,
Norton, she has had no wood to make a fire
even to boil her kettle."

" And no kettle to boil," added Norton.

" So that she went without even tea. I don't know how she lived. Did you see how she enjoyed the tea yesterday?"

" Pink," said Norton, " do you expect to go there to make her fire every day?"

" No, Norton, I cannot every day; I cannot always get away from home. But I was thinking — I know some other girls that I guess would help; and if there were several of us, you know, it would be very easy."

" Well," said Norton, " we have fixed up this palace and princess now. What do you think of getting the princess a new dress or two?"

" O it would be very nice, Norton. She wants it."

" Mamma will do that. Could *you* get it, Pink? would you know how? supposing your purse was long enough."

" O yes, Norton. Of course I could!"

" Then you shall do it. Who will see to all the rest?"

"To buy the things, do you mean?"

"To buy them, and to choose them, and to get them to their place, and all that?"

"Why, you and I, Norton. Shan't we?"

"I think that is a good arrangement. The next question is, when? When shall we send the things there?"

"We must get the rooms cleaned. I will see about that. Then, Norton, the sooner the better; don't you think so?"

"How is it in the fairy stories?"

"O, it's all done with a breath there; that is one of the delightful things about it. You speak, and the genie comes; and you tell him what you want, and he goes and fetches it; there is no waiting. And yet, I don't know," Matilda added; "I don't wish this could be done in a breath" —

"What?" said a voice close behind her. The two looked up, laughing, to see Mrs. Laval. She was laughing too.

"What is it, that is not to be done in a breath?"

" Furnishing a palace, mamma — (getting it cleaned first,) and setting up a princess."

Mrs. Laval wanted to hear about it, and gradually she slipped down on the grass beside Matilda and drew an arm round her, while she listened to Norton's story. Norton made quite a story of it, and told his mother what Matilda had been doing the day before in Lilac lane, and what schemes they had presently on hand. Mrs. Laval listened curiously.

" Dear, is it quite safe for you to go to such a place ? " she asked Matilda then.

" O yes, ma'am."

" But it cannot be pleasant."

" O yes, ma'am ! " Matilda answered more earnestly.

" How can it be ? "

" I thought it would not be pleasant, at first," said Matilda. " But I found it was."

" What made it pleasant, dear ? "

" If you saw the poor old woman, Mrs.

Laval, and how much she wanted comfort, I think you would understand it."

" Would you come and see *me*, if I wanted comfort?" the lady inquired. Matilda smiled at the possibility. Then something in Mrs. Laval's face reminded her that even with such a beautiful house and so rich abundance of things that money can buy, there might be a sad want of something that money cannot buy; and she grew grave again.

" Would you?" Mrs. Laval repeated.

And Matilda said yes. And Mrs. Laval again put her face down to Matilda's face and pressed her lips upon hers, again and again, as if she drew some sweetness from them. Not so passionately as the time before; yet with quiet earnestness. Then with one hand she stroked the hair from Matilda's forehead, and drew it forward, and passed her fingers through it; caressing it in a tender, thoughtful way. Norton knelt on the grass beside them and looked on, watching and satisfied. Matilda was happy and passive.

" Have you got money enough, love, for all you want to do ? " Mrs. Laval asked at length.

" *I* haven't much," said Matilda ; "but Norton is going to help."

" Have you got enough, Norton ? "

" I guess so, mamma."

Mrs. Laval put her hand in her pocket and drew out a little morocco pocket-book. She put it in Matilda's hand.

" Norton shall not do it all," she said. " I don't know exactly how much is in this ; you can use what you choose on this fairy palace you and Norton are building."

" O ma'am ! " Matilda began, flushing and delighted. Mrs. Laval stopped her mouth with a kiss.

" But ma'am — won't you please take out what you wish I should spend for Mrs. Eldridge " —

" Spend just what you like."

" I might take too much," said Matilda.

" It is all your's. Do just what you like

with it. Spend what you like in Lilac lane, and the rest for something else."

"O ma'am!" — Matilda began again in utter bewildered delight.

"No, darling, don't say anything about it," Mrs. Laval answered, finding Matilda's pocket and slipping the pocket-book in. "You shall talk to me about it another time. I wish you could give me your secret."

"What secret, ma'am?" said Matilda, who for the very delight that flushed her could hardly speak.

"How to get so much satisfaction out of a little money."

Matilda wished she could give Mrs. Laval anything that would do her a pleasure; and she began to think, *could* she let her into this secret? It seemed a simple secret enough to Matilda; but she had a certain consciousness that for the great lady it might be more difficult to understand than it was for her. Was it possible that elegant pocket-book was in *her* pocket?

But now came the summons to tea, and they got up off the grass and went in. So beautiful a table Matilda had never seen; and more thorough petting no little girl ever had. No one else was there but those three, so she was quite at home. Such a pleasant home it was, too. The windows all open, of the large, airy, pretty dining room; the blue mountains seen through the windows at one side; from the others, the green of the trees and the gay colours of flowers; the evening air drew gently through the room; and flowers and fruit and all sorts of delicacies and all sorts of elegances on the table made Matilda feel she was in fairyland.

" When are you coming again ? " said Mrs. Laval, taking her in her arms when she was about going.

" Whenever you will let me, ma'am."

" Could you learn to love me a little bit, some day ? "

Matilda did not know how to answer. She looked into the handsome dark eyes that were watching her, and with the thought of the secret sympathy between the lady and herself, her own watered.

"I see you will," said Mrs. Laval kissing her. "Now kiss me."

She sat quite still while Matilda did so; then returned it warmly, and bade Norton take care of her home.

CHAPTER V.

MATILDA found her aunt, cousin and sister gathered in the parlour.

"Well!" said Maria. "I suppose you have had a time."

"A good time?" Mrs. Candy asked. Matilda replied yes.

"You staid late," observed Clarissa. This did not seem to need an answer.

"What have you been doing?" Maria asked.

"Playing."

"You sigh over it, as if there were some melancholy associations connected with the fact," said Clarissa.

So there were, taken with the contrast at home. Matilda could not explain that.

"Any company there?" inquired Mrs. Candy.

" No, ma'am."

" You are wonderfully taciturn," said Clarissa. " Do tell us what you have been about, and whether you have enjoyed yourself."

" I enjoyed myself," said Matilda, repressing another sigh.

" Did you bring any message for me?" asked her aunt.

" No, aunt Candy."

" Did you deliver mine to Mrs. Laval?"

" What, ma'am ? "

" My message.   Did you deliver it ?"

" No, aunt Candy."

" Did you forget it, Matilda ? "

" I did not forget it."

Both mother and daughter lifted up their heads at this.

" Why did you not give the message then ? "

Matilda was in sore difficulty.   There was nothing she could think of to say.   So she said nothing.

" Speak, child ! " said her aunt. " Why did you not give my message as I charged you?"

"I did not like to do it, aunt Candy.

" You did not like to do it! Please to say why you did not like to do it."

It was so impossible to answer, that Matilda took refuge in silence again.

" It would have been civil in Mrs. Laval to have sent her message, whether or no," said Clarissa.

" Go upstairs, Matilda," said her aunt ; " and don't come down again to-night. No, Maria," for Maria rose, muttering that she would go too, — " no, you do *not* go now. Sit down — till the usual time. Go to bed, Matilda. I will talk to you to-morrow."

It was no punishment, the being sent off; though her aunt's words and manner were. In all her little life, till now, Matilda had never known any but gentle and tender treatment. She had not been a child to require other; and though a more decided government might have been good, perhaps, the soft and easy affection in the midst of which she had grown up was far better for her than harshness, which indeed she never deserved. As she went up the stairs to-night, she felt like a person suddenly removed in the space of an hour from the atmosphere of some balmy, tropical clime, to the sharp rigours of the north pole. She shivered, mentally.

But the effect of the tropics returned when she had closed the door of her room. The treasures of comfort and pleasure stored up that afternoon were not lost; and being a secret treasure, they were not within anybody's power. Matilda kneeled down and gave thanks for it all; then took out her pocket-book and admired it; she would not count the money this evening, the outside was quite enough. She stowed it away in a safe place, and slowly undressed; her heart so full of pleasant things enjoyed and other pleasant things hoped for, that she soon utterly forgot Mrs. Candy, message and all.

Sweet visions of. what was to be done in Lilac lane rose before her eyes; what might *not* be done, between Norton and her, now? and with these came in other visions; of those kisses of Mrs. Laval, which had been such mother's kisses. Matilda stood still to remember and feel them over again. Nobody had ever kissed her so, but her mother. And so, in a little warm heart-glow of her own which enveloped everything, like the golden haze on the mountains that evening, Matilda undressed leisurely, and read her Bible, and prayed, and went to sleep. And her waking mood was like the morning light upon the mountains, so clear and quiet.

Maria, however, was in complete contrast. This was not very unusual. She was crusty, and ironical, and disposed to find fault.

"I wonder how long this is going to last?" she said, in the interval between complaining and fault-finding.

"What?" Matilda asked.

"This state of things. Not going to

school, nor learning anything; cooking and scrubbing for aunt Candy; and you petted and taken upstairs to be taught, and asked out to tea, and made much of. Nobody remembers that I am alive."

"Dear Maria, I have been asked out to tea just once."

"You'll be asked again."

"And I am sure people come to see you. Frances Barth was here yesterday; and Sarah Haight and Esther Trembleton two days ago; and Esther asked you to tea too."

"I couldn't go."

"But people remember you are alive. O, Maria, they remember you too. Mr. Richmond don't forget you; and Miss Benton asked you to come to tea with her."

"It is all very well talking," said Maria. "I know what I know; and I am getting tired of it. You are the only one that has any really good times."

It soon appeared that one of Matilda's good times was not to be to-day. Mrs. Candy and Clarissa looked on her coldly, spoke to her dryly, and made her feel that she was not in favour. Matilda could bear this down-stairs pretty well; but when she found her-self in Mrs. Candy's room for her morning hours of reading and darning, it became heavy. Reading was not the first thing to-day. Mrs. Candy called Matilda to stand before her while she proceeded to give her a species of correction in words.

" You were baptized a few weeks ago, Matilda."

" Yes, ma'am."

" And by so being, you became a member of the church ; — of your church."

" Yes, ma'am."

" What do you think are the duties of a member of the church ? "

A comprehensive question, Matilda thought. She hesitated.

" I ask you, what do you think are the duties of a member of the church ? in any branch of it."

" I suppose they are the same as anybody else's duties," Matilda answered.

" The same as anybody else's duties."

" Yes, aunt Candy."

" You think it makes no change in one's duties ? "

" What change does it make, aunt Candy ? "

Matilda spoke in all innocence; but Mrs. Candy flushed and frowned. It did not sweeten her mood, that she could not readily find an answer for the child.

" You allow, at least, that it is *one* of your duties to obey the fifth commandment ? "

" Yes, aunt Candy.   I try to do it."

" Did you try last night ? "

Matilda was silent.

" You made me guilty of rudeness by not delivering the message I had charged you with ; and you confessed it was not through forgetfulness.   Will you tell me now why it was ? "

It had been through a certain nice sense on

Matilda's part that the message was uncalled for, and even a little officious. She would have been mortified to be obliged to repeat it to Mrs. Laval. There had never been the least intercourse between the ladies, and Mrs. Laval had sought none. If Mrs. Candy sought it, Matilda was unwilling it should be through her means. But she could not explain this to her aunt.

"You did not choose it," that lady said again, with kindling anger.

"I did not mean to offend you, aunt Candy."

"No, because you thought I would never hear of it. I have a great mind, as ever I had to eat, to whip you, Matilda. You are not at all too old for it, and I believe it would do you a great deal of good. You haven't had quite enough of that sort of thing."

Whether Matilda had or had not had enough of that sort of thing, it seemed to her that it was very far from Mrs. Candy's place to propose or even hint at it. The indignity of the proposal flushed the child with a sense of injury almost too strong to be borne. Mrs. Candy, in all her years of life, had never known the sort of keen pain that her words gave now to a sensitive nature, up to that time held in the most dainty and tender consideration. Matilda did not speak nor stir; but she grew pale.

"The next time you shall have it," Mrs. Candy went on. "I should have no hesitation at all, Matilda, about whipping you; and my hand is not a light one. I advise you as your friend not to come under it. Your present punishment shall be, that I shall refuse you permission to go any more to Mrs. Laval's."

The child was motionless and gave no sign, further than the paleness of her cheeks which indeed caught Clarissa's observant eye and made her uneasy. But she did not tremble nor weep. Probably the rush of feeling made such a storm in her little breast that she could not accurately measure the value of this new announcement, or know fairly what it meant. Perhaps too it was like some other things to her limited experience, too bad to be believed; and Matilda did not really receive it as a fact, that her visits to Mrs. Laval had ceased. She realized enough, however, poor child, to make it extremely difficult to bear up and maintain her dignity; but she did that. Nothing but the paleness told. Matilda was quite erect and steady before her aunt; and when she was at last bidden to go to her seat and begin her reading, her graceful little head took a set upon her shoulders which was very incensing to Mrs. Candy.

"I advise you to take care!" she said threateningly.

But Matilda could not imagine what new cause of offence she had given. It was very hard to read aloud! She made two or three efforts to get voice, and then went stiffly on.

" You are not reading well," her aunt broke

in. "You are not thinking of what you are reading."

Matilda was silent.

"Why do you not speak? I say you do not read well. Why don't you attend to your book?"

"I never understand this book," said Matilda.

"Of course not, if you do not attend. Go on!"

"She can't read, mamma," whispered Clarissa.

"She shall read," Mrs. Candy returned in an answering whisper.

And recognizing that necessity, Matilda put a force on herself and read on; at the imminent peril of choking every now and then, as one thought and another came up to grasp her. She put it by or put it down, and went on; obliged herself to go on; wouldn't think; till the weary pages were come to an end at last, and the hoarse voice had leave to be still, and she took up her darning.   Thoughts would have overcome her self-control then, in all nature; but that, happily for Matilda's dignity as she wished to maintain it, Mrs. Candy was pleased to interrupt the darning of stockings to give Matilda a lesson in patching linen.   An entirely new thing to the child, requiring her best attention and care; for Mrs. Candy insisted upon the patch being straight to a thread, and even as a double web would have been. Matilda had to baste and take out again, baste and take out again; she had enough to do without going back upon her own grievances; it was extremely difficult to make a large patch of linen lie straight on all sides and not pucker itself · or the cloth somewhere.   Matilda pulled out her basting threads the third time, with a sigh.

" You will do it, when you come to taking pains enough," said Mrs. Candy.

Now Matilda knew that she was taking the utmost pains possible.   She said nothing, but her hands grew more unsteady.

"Mamma, may I help her?" said Clarissa.

"No.   She can do it if she tries," said Mrs. Candy.

Matilda queried within herself, how it would do, to throw up the work and declare open rebellion; how would the fight go? She was conscious that to provoke a fight would be wrong; but passion just now had got the upper hand of wisdom in the child. She concluded however that it would not do; Mrs. Candy could hold out better than she could; but the last atom of good will was gone out of her obedience.

"Matilda" — said Mrs. Candy.

"Yes, ma'am."

"You have been an hour and a half trying to fix that patch."

"Isn't it long enough for one day?" said Matilda wearily, sitting back on her heels.

She had got down on the floor the better to manage the work; a large garment with a large patch to be laid.

"Too long, by an hour; but not long enough, inasmuch as it is not yet done."

"I am too tired to do it."

"We will see that."

Matilda sat back on her heels, looking at the hopeless piece of linen. She was flushed and tired and angry, but she only sat there looking at the linen.

"It has got to be done," said Mrs. Candy.

"I must get rested first," said Matilda.

"You are not to say 'must' to me," said her aunt. "My dear, I shall make you do whatever I order. You shall do exactly what I tell you in everything. Your times of having your own way are ended. You will do my way now. And you will put on that patch neatly before you eat."

"Maria will want me."

"Maria will do very well without."

Matilda looked at her aunt in equal surprise and dismay. Mrs. Candy had not seemed like this before. Nothing had prepared her for it. But Mrs. Candy was a cold-natured woman, not the less fiery and proud when roused. She could be pleasant enough on the surface and in general intercourse with people; she could have petted Matilda and made much of her, and was indeed quite inclined that way. If only Mrs. Laval had not taken her up, and if Matilda had not been so independent. The two things together touched her on the wrong side. She was nettled that the wish of Mrs. Laval was to see only Matilda, of the whole family; and upon the back of that, she was displeased beyond endurance that Matilda should withstand her authority and differ from her opinion. There was no fine and delicate nature in her, to read that of the child; only a coarse pride that was bent upon having itself regarded. She thought herself disregarded. She was determined to put that down with a high hand.

Seeing or feeling dimly somewhat of all this, Matilda sat on the floor in a kind of despair, looking at her patch.

" You had better not sit so but go about it," said Mrs. Candy.

" Yes. I am tired," said Matilda.

" You will not go-down to dinner," said Mrs. Candy.

Could she stand it? Matilda thought. Could she bear it, and not cry? She was getting so tired and downhearted. It was quite plain there would be no going out this afternoon to buy things for Lilac lane. That delightful shopping must be postponed. That hope was put further in the distance. She sat moodily still. She ceased to care when the patching got done.

" Losing time," said Mrs. Candy at length, getting up and putting by her own basket. " The bell will ring in a few minutes, Matilda; and I shall leave you here to do your work at your leisure."

The child looked at her and looked down again, with what slight air of her little head it is impossible to describe, though it undoubtedly and unmistakably signified her disapproval. It was Matilda's habitual gesture, but resented by Mrs. Candy. She stepped up to her and gave the side of her head a smart stroke with the palm of her hand.

" You are not to answer me by gestures, you know I told you," she exclaimed. And she and Clarissa quitting the room, the door was locked on the outside.

Matilda's condition at first was one of simple bewilderment.. The indignity, the injury, the wrong, were so unwonted and so unintelligible, that the child felt as if she were in a dream. What did it mean? and was it real? The locked door was a hard fact, that constantly asserted itself; perhaps so did Matilda's want of dinner; the linen patches on the floor were another tangible fact. And as Matilda came to realize that she was alone and could indulge herself, at last a flood of bitter tears came to wash, they could not wash away, her hurt feeling and her despair. Every bond was broken, to Matilda's thinking, between her and her aunt; all friendship

was gone that had been from one to the other; and she was in the power of one who would use it. That was the hardest to realize; for if Matilda had been in her mother's power once, it had also been power never exercised. The child had been always practically her own mistress. Was that ended? Was Mrs. Candy her mistress now? her freedom gone? and was there no escape? It made Matilda almost wild to think these thoughts, wild and frightened together. And with all that, very angry. Not passionately, which was not her nature, but with a deep sense of displeasure and dislike. The patch and the linen to be patched lay untouched on the floor, it is needless to say, when Mrs. Candy came up from dinner.

Mrs. Candy came up alone. She surveyed the state of things in silence. Matilda had been crying, she saw. She left her time to recover from that and take up her work. But Matilda sat despairing and careless, looking at it and not thinking of it.

" You do not mean to do that, do you?" she said at last.

" Yes, ma'am — some time," Matilda answered.

" Not now?"

" When I get a little rested."

" You want something," said Mrs. Candy looking at her; "and I know what it is. You want bringing down. You never were brought down in your life, I believe, or you would not dare me so now!"

" I did not mean to dare you, aunt Candy," said Matilda lifting her head.

" You will not do it after to-day," said Mrs. Candy. "I am not going to give you what I threatened. I leave that for another time. I don't believe we shall ever come to that. But you want bringing down, all the same; and I know what will do it too. Cold water will do it."

" What do you mean, aunt Candy?"

" I. mean cold water. I have heard you say you don't like it, but it would be very good for you, in two ways. I am going to bathe you with it from your head to your feet. Here is my bath tub, and I'll have it ready in a minute. Take off your clothes, Matilda."

It was with nothing less than horror that Matilda now earnestly besought her aunt to think better of this determination. She did dislike cold water, and after a child's luxurious fashion had always been allowed to use warm water. But worse than cold water was the idea of her aunt, or anybody, presuming to apply it in the capacity of bather. Matilda refused and pleaded, alternately; pleaded very humbly at last; but in vain.

" I thought I knew something that would bring you down," Mrs. Candy said composedly and pleased; and in the same manner proceeded to strip off Matilda's clothes, put her in the bath tub, and make thorough application of the hated element as she had said, from head to foot; scrubbing and dousing and sponging; till if Matilda had been in the sea she would not better have known how cold water felt all over her. It was done in five minutes too; and then after being well rubbed down, Matilda was directed to put on her clothes again and finish her patching.

"I fancy you will feel refreshed for it now," said her aunt. "This will be a good thing for you. I used to give it to Clarissa always when she was a little thing; and now I will do the same by you, my love. Every day, you shall come to me in the morning when you first get up."

No announcement could have been more dismayful; but this time Matilda said nothing. She bent herself to her patching, the one uppermost desire being to finish it and get out of the room. The cold water *had* refreshed and strengthened her, much as she disliked and hated it; at the same time the sense of hunger, from the same cause, grew keener than ever. Matilda tried her very best to lay the patch straight and get it basted so. And so keen the endeavour was, so earnest the attention, that though laying a linen patch by the thread *is* a nice piece of business, she succeeded at last. Mrs. Candy was content with the work, satisfied with its being only basted for that time, and let her go.

Matilda slowly made her way down to the lower regions, where Maria was still at work, and asked for something to eat. Maria looked very black, and demanded explanations of what was going on upstairs. Matilda would say nothing, until she had found something to satisfy her hunger and had partially devoured a slice of bread and meat. In the midst of that she broke off, and wrapping her arms round her sister in a clinging way, exclaimed suddenly, —

"O Maria, keep me, keep me!"

"Keep you! from what? What do you mean, Tilly?" said the astonished Maria.

"From aunt Candy. *Can't* you keep me?"

"What has she done?" Maria asked, growing very wrathful.

" Can't you keep me from her, Maria ? "

" And I say, what has she done to you, Tilly ? Do hold up and answer me. How can I tell anything when you act like that? What has she done ? "

" She says she'll give me a cold bath every morning," Matilda said, seeming to shrink and shiver as she said it.

" A cold bath ! " exclaimed Maria.

" Yes. O can't you keep me from it ? "

" What has put the notion in her head ? "

" She used to do it to Clarissa, she says; but I think she wants to do it to me because I don't like it. O I don't like it, Maria ! " —

" She's too mean for anything," said Maria. " I never saw anything like her. But maybe it won't be so bad as you think, Tilly. She and Clarissa both take a cold bath every morning, you know; and they like it."

" I don't like it ! " said Matilda with the extremest accent of repugnance.

" Maybe it won't seem so bad when you've tried."

" I *have* tried," said Matilda bursting into tears; " she gave me one to-day; and I don't like it; and I can't *bear* to have her bathe me!"

Matilda's tears came now in a shower, with sobs of the most heartfelt trouble. Maria looked black as a thunder cloud.

" O Maria, can't you keep me from her?"

" Not without killing her," said Maria. "I feel as if I would almost like to do that some-times."

" O Maria, you mustn't speak so!" said Matilda, shocked even in the midst of her grief.

" Well and I don't mean it," said Maria; " but what can I do, Tilly? If she takes a notion in her head, she will follow it, you know; and it would take more than ever I saw to turn her. And you see, she thinks cold water is the best thing in the world."

" Yes, but I *can't* bear to have her bathe me!" Matilda repeated. " And I don't like cold water. She rubs, and she scrubs, and she throws the water over me, and the soap-suds, and she don't care at all whether I like it or not. I wish I could get away! I wish I could get away, Maria! O I wish I could get away!"

"So do I wish I could," said Maria, gloomily eyeing her little sister's sobs. "We've got to stand it, Tilly, for the present. I haven't anywhere to go to, and you haven't. Come, don't cry. Eat your bread and meat. I dare say you will get used to cold water."

"I shall not get used to *her*," said Matilda.

However, a part of Maria's prediction did come true. Cold water is less terrible, the more acquaintance one has with it; and probably Mrs. Candy's assertion was also true, that it was capital for Matilda. And Matilda would not have much minded it at last, if only the administration could have been left to herself. But Mrs. Candy kept that in her own hands, knowing probably that it was one effectual means of keeping Matilda herself in her hands. Every morning, when

Mrs. Candy's bell rang, Matilda was obliged to run downstairs and submit herself to her aunt's manipulations, which were pretty much as she had described them; and under those energetic unscrupulous hands, which dealt with her as they listed and regarded her wishes in no sort nor respect, Matilda was quite helpless. And she was subdued. Mrs. Candy had attained that end. She no longer thought of resisting her aunt in any way. It was the first time in Matilda's life that she had been obliged to obey another. Between her mother and herself the question had hardly arisen, except upon isolated occasions. She dared not let the question ever arise now with Mrs. Candy. She read, and darned, and patched, and grew skilful in those latter arts; she never objected now. She came to her bath, and never uttered now the vain pleadings which at first even her dignity gave way to make. Mrs. Candy had quite put down the question of dignity. Matilda did not venture to disobey her any more in anything. She went no more to walk without asking leave; she visited no more at Mrs. Laval's; Mrs. Candy even took Matilda in her triumph to her own church in the morning. Matilda suffered, but submitted without a word.

How much the child suffered, nobody knew or guessed. She kept it to herself. Mrs. Candy did not even suspect that there was much suffering in the case, beyond a little enforced submission, and a little disappointment now and then about going to see somebody. Mrs. Laval's ·house was forbidden, that was all; and for a few days Matilda did not get time, or leave, to go out to walk.

She was kept very busy. And she was pleasant about her work with Maria, and gentle and well-behaved when at her work with her aunt. Not gay, certainly, as she had begun to be sometimes lately, before this time; but Maria was so far from gayety herself that she did not miss it in her sister; and Mrs. Candy saw no change but the change she had wished for. Nevertheless they did not see all. There were hours, when Matilda could shut herself up in her room and be alone, and Maria was asleep in her bed at night; when the little head bent over her Bible, and tears fell like rain, and struggles that nobody dreamed of went on in the child's heart. The thing she lived on, was the hope of getting out and doing that beloved shopping; meeting Norton somehow, somewhere, as one does impossible things in a dream, and arranging with him to go to Lilac lane together. The little pocket-book lay all safe and ready waiting for the time; and when Matilda could let herself think pleasant thoughts, she went into rapturous fancies of the wonderful changes to be wrought in Mrs. Eldridge's house.

She saw nothing meanwhile of Lemuel Dow. The Sunday following her afternoon at Mrs. Laval's had been a little rainy in the latter part of it. Perhaps the little Dow boy, who minded rain no more than a duck ou other days, might be afraid of a wetting on Sunday. Other people often are. But Matilda meant to look for him next time, and have her sugared almonds in readiness.

One of the days of that week, it happened that Mrs. Candy took Matilda out with her for a walk. It was not at all agreeable to Matilda; but she was learning to submit to what was not agreeable, and she made no objection. On the way they stopped at Mr. Sample's store; Mrs. Candy wanted to get some smoked salmon. Mr. Sample served her himself.

"How did you like the tea I sent you?" he asked while he was weighing the fish.

"Tea?" said Mrs. Candy. "You sent me no tea."

"Why yes I did; last week; it was Monday or Tuesday, I think. You wanted to try another kind, I understood."

"I wanted nothing of the sort. I have plenty of tea on hand, and am perfectly suited with it. You have made some mistake."

"I am glad you are suited," Mr. Sample rejoined; "but I have made no mistake. This little girl came for it, and I weighed it out myself and gave it to her. And a loaf of bread at the same time."

"It was not for you, aunt Candy; it was for myself," said Matilda. "I paid for it, Mr. Sample; it was not charged."

" You did not pay me, Miss Matilda."

" No, Mr. Sample; I paid Patrick."

" What did you buy tea and bread for?" her aunt inquired.

" I wanted it " — Matilda answered.

" What for ? "

"I wanted it to give away," Matilda said in a low voice, being obliged to speak.

Mrs. Candy waited till they were out of the shop, and then desired to know particulars. For whom Matilda wanted it; where she took it; when she went; who went with her.

" Is it a clean place ? " was her inquiry at last. Matilda was obliged to confess it was not.

"Don't go there again without my knowledge, Matilda. Do you hear?"

"I hear. But aunt Candy," said Matilda in great dismay, "it doesn't hurt me."

"No. I mean it shall not. Have you always gone wandering just where you liked?"

"Yes, always. Shadywalk is a perfectly safe place."

"For common children perhaps. Not for you. Do not go near Lilac lane again. It is a mercy you have escaped safe as it is."

Escaped from what, Matilda wondered? Even a little soil to her clothes might be washed off; and she did not think she had got so much harm as that. If she could only meet Norton, now, before reaching home! there would never be another chance. Matilda longed to see him, with an intensity which seemed almost as if it must bring him before her; but it did not. In vain she watched every corner and every group of boys or cluster of people they passed; Norton's trim figure was not to be seen; and the house door shut upon Matilda in her despair. She went up to her room, and kneeling down laid her head on the table.

"It's almost tea-time," said Maria. "What is the matter now?"

But Matilda was not crying; she was in despair.

"Come!" said Maria. "Come, what ails you? Tired?—It is time to get tea, Matilda, and I want your help. What *is* the matter now?"

Matilda lifted a perfectly forlorn face to her sister.

"I can't go anywhere!" she said. "I am in prison. I can't go to Lilac lane any more. I cannot do anything any more. And they want me so!"—

Down went Matilda's head. Maria stood, perhaps a little conscience struck.

"*Who* wants you so much?"

"The poor people there. Mrs. Eldridge and Mrs. Rogers. They want me so much."

"What for, Tilly?" said Maria, a little more gently than her wont.

"O for a great many things," said Matilda, brushing away a tear or two; "and now I can go no more — I cannot do anything — O dear!"

The little girl broke down.

"She's the most hateful, spiteful, masterful woman, that ever was!" Maria exclaimed; "too mean to live, and too cunning to breathe. She's an old witch!"

"O don't, Maria!"

"I will," said Maria. "I will talk. It is the only comfort I have. What is she up to now?"

"Just that," said Matilda. "She found I had been to Lilac lane, and she said I must not go again without her knowing; and she will never let me go. I needn't ask her. She doesn't like me to go there. And I wanted to do so much! If she could only have waited — only have waited" —

"What made you let her know you had been there?"

" She found out.   I couldn't help it.   Now she will not let me go ever again.   Never, never ! "

" What did you want to do in Lilac lane, Tilly ? "

" O, things.   I wanted to do a great deal. Things. — They'll never be done ! " cried Matilda in bitter distress.   " I cannot do them now.   I cannot do anything."

" She is as mean as she can live ! " said Maria again.   " But Tilly, I don't believe Lilac lane is a good place for you, neither. What did you want to do there?   what *could* you do ? "

" Things " — said Matilda, indefinitely. ·

" You are not old enough to go poking about Lilac lane by yourself."

" I can't go any way," said Matilda.

She cried a long while to wash down this disappointment; and the effects of it did not go off in the tears.   The child became very silent and sober.   Her duties she did, as she had done them, about the house and in Mrs.

Candy's room; but the bright face and the glad ways were gone. In the secret of her private hours Matilda had struggles to go through that left her with the marks of care upon her all the rest of the time.

The next Sunday she was made to go to church with her aunt. She went to her own Sunday school in the afternoon; but she was not allowed to get off early enough for the reading and talk with Mary and Ailie. Lem Dow however was on hand; that was one single drop of comfort. He looked for his sugared almonds, and they were on hand too; and besides that, Matilda was able to see that he was quite pleased with the place and the singing and the doings in his class, and making friends with the boys.

"Will you come next Sunday?" Matilda asked him as they were going out. He nodded.

"Won't Jemima come too, if you ask her?"

"I won't ask her."

"No? why not?"

" I don't want her to come."

" You don't want her to come?   Why it is a pleasant place, isn't it ? "

" It's a heap more jolly if she ain't here," said Lem knowingly.

It was a difficult argument to answer, with one whose general benevolence was not very full grown yet.   Matilda went home thinking how many people wanted something done for them, and how she could touch nobody. She was not allowed to go to church in the evening.

CHAPTER VI.

THE days seemed to move slowly. They were such troublesome days to Matilda. From the morning bath, which was simply her detestation, all through the long hours of reading and patching and darning in Mrs. Candy's room, the time dragged; and no sooner was dinner over than she began to dread the next morning again. It was not so much for the cold water as for the relentless hand that applied it. Matilda greatly resented having it applied to her at all by any hand but her own; it was an aggravation that her aunt minded that, and her, no more than if she had been a baby. It was a daily trial, and daily trouble; for Matilda was obliged to conquer herself, and be silent, and submit, where her whole soul rose and rebelled

She must not speak her anger, and pleadings were entirely disregarded. So she ran down in the morning when her aunt's bell rang, and was passive under all that Mrs. Candy pleased to inflict; and commanded herself when she wanted to cry for vexation, and was still when words of entreaty or defiance rose to her lips. The sharp lesson of self-control Matilda was learning now. She had to practise it again when she took her hours of needlework. Mrs. Candy was teaching her now to knit, and now to mend lace, and then to make buttonholes; and she required perfection; and Matilda was forced to be very patient, and careful to the extreme of carefulness, and docile when her work was pulled out, and persevering when she was quite tired and longed to go down and help Maria in the kitchen. She was learning useful arts, no doubt, but Matilda did not care for them; all the while the most valuable thing she was learning was the lesson of power over herself. Well if that were all. But there were some things also down in the bottom of Matilda's heart which it was not good to learn; and she knew it; but she did not know very well how to help it.

Several weeks had gone by in this manner, and now June was about over. Matilda had not gone to Lilac lane again, nor seen Norton, nor made any of her purchases for Mrs. Eldridge. She had almost given all that up. She wondered that she saw nothing of Norton; but if he had ever come to the house she had not heard of it. Matilda was not allowed to go out in the evening now any more. No more Band meetings or prayer meetings or church service in the evening for her. And in the morning of Sunday Mrs. Candy was very apt to carry her off to her own church, which Matilda disliked beyond all expression. But she went as quietly as if she had liked it.

Things were in this state, when one evening Maria came up to bed and burst out as soon as she had got into the room, —

" Think of it! They are going to New York to-morrow."

Matilda was bewildered, and asked who was going to New York.

" *They.* Aunt Erminia and Clarissa. To be gone all day! Hurra! We'll have just what we like for dinner, and I'll let the kitchen fire go out."

" Are they going down to New York to-morrow?" said Matilda, standing and looking at her sister.

" By the early train.. Don't you hear me tell you?"

" I thought it was too good news to be true," said Matilda drawing a long breath.

." It is, almost; but they are going. They are going to do shopping. That's what it's for. And I say, Matilda, won't we have a great dinner to get!"

" They will want dinner after 'they get home."

" No they won't. They will take dinner somehow down there. Why they will not be home, Tilly, till nine o'clock. They can't. The train don't get up till a quarter past eight, that train they are going to take; and they will have to be an hour pretty near riding up from the station. Hurra! hurra!"

"Hush! don't make so much noise. They will hear you."

"No they won't. They have come up to bed. We are to have breakfast at six o'clock. We shall have all the longer day."

"Then I hope aunt Candy will not have time to give me my bath."

"No, she won't; she told me to tell you. You are to be ever so early, and help me to get the breakfast. I shall not know what to do with the day, though, I shall want to do so much. That is the worst of it."

Matilda thought *she* would be under no such difficulty, if only her way were not so hedged in. The things she would have liked to do were forbidden things. She might not go to Lilac lane; she might not go to Mrs. Laval's. She half expected that her aunt would say she must not go out of the house at all. That misfortune however did not happen. The early breakfast and bustle and arrangements for getting off occupied Mrs. Candy so completely that she gave no commands whatever. The omnibus fairly drove away with her and left Maria and Matilda unrestricted by any new restrictions.

"It seems," said Matilda gravely, as they stood by the gate, "it seems as if I could see the sky again. I haven't seen it this great while."

"Seen the sky!" said Maria; "what has ailed you? You have gone out often enough."

"It didn't seem as if I could see the sky," said Matilda, gazing up into the living blue depth above her. "I can see it now."

"You are funny," said Maria. "It don't seem to me as if I had seen anything, for weeks. Dear me! to-day will be only too short."

"It is half past six now," said Matilda.

" Between now and nine o'clock to-night there are — let me see; half past twelve will be six hours, and half past six will be twelve hours; six, seven, eight, nine, — nine will be two hours and a half more; that will be fourteen and a half hours."

" Fourteen," said Maria. " That half we shall be expecting them."

" Well, we've got to go in and put the house in order, first thing," said Matilda. " Let's make haste."

" Then I'll let the kitchen fire go out," said Maria; " and we'll dine on bread and butter and cold potatoes. I like cold potatoes; don't you?"

" No," said Matilda; " but I don't care what we have. I'll have bread and butter and cold coffee, Maria; let us save the coffee. That will do."

With these arrangements made, the day began. The two girls flew round in a kind of glee to put the rooms up and get all the work done out of the way. Work was a kind of play that morning. Then they agreed to take their dinner early and dress themselves. Maria was going out after that to see some friends and have some fun, she said. Matilda on her part had a sort of faint hope that to-day, when it would be so opportune, it might happen that Norton Laval would come to see what had become of her. She was almost afraid to go out, and lose the chance; though to be sure it was only the ghost of a chance. Yet for that ghost of a chance she did linger and wait in the house for an hour or two after Maria had gone out. Then it began to press upon her, that her aunt had ordered her to get some strawberries from Mr. Sample's for tea; she was uneasy till it was done; and at last took her hat and her basket and resolved to run round into Butternut street and get that off her mind.

She was standing in Mr. Sample's shop, patiently waiting until her turn should come to be served, when a hand was laid upon her shoulder.

"How do you do, Tilly? You are grown a stranger."

"O Mr. Richmond!" was Matilda's startled response. And it was more startled than glad.

"What is the matter? you look as if I had frightened you, — almost," said the minister smiling. Matilda did not say what was the matter.

"Have you been quite well?"

"Yes, sir."

"You were not in your place on Sunday."

"No, sir."

And Matilda's tone of voice gave an unconscious commentary upon her very few words.

"And you have not been to take tea with me in a great while."

"No, Mr. Richmond."

"Suppose you come to-day."

"O I cannot, sir."

"Why not? I think you can."

"I don't know whether my aunt would let me."

"We will go and ask her."

"O no, sir; she is not at home, Mr. Richmond. She has gone to New York."

"For how long?"

"Only till nine o'clock to-night."

"Then there can be no possible harm in your coming to take tea at the parsonage."

"I don't know whether she would let me," said Matilda, with an evident intimation that the doubt was barrier enough.

"You think she would not like it?"

"I think — perhaps — she would not. Thank you, Mr. Richmond!"

"But Tilly, I want to talk to you. Have you nothing to say to me?"

"Yes, sir. A great deal," said the child with the look of slow meditation. The minister considered her for a moment.

"I shall take the decision of the question upon myself, Tilly, and I will make it all right with your aunt. Come to the parsonage, or rather, go to the parsonage; and I will join you there presently. I have half an hour's business first to attend to. You must carry those strawberries home? Very well; then go straight to the parsonage and wait there for me."

And with an encouraging nod and smile, Mr. Richmond walked off. Matilda took her basket home; carried the key of the house door to Maria at Mrs. Trembleton's; and set her face up Butternut street.

She was very glad; it seemed like getting out of prison; though she was not altogether satisfied in her mind that Mr. Richmond might be able to make it all right with Mrs. Candy. She was obliged to risk that, for Mr. Richmond's invitation had had the force of an injunction. So she took the good of the moment, and turned in at the gate of the parsonage lane with something like a feeling of exultation and triumph. The shadow of the elms was sweet on the road; the smooth quiet of the grounds, railed off from worldly business and care, seemed proper only to the houses of peace which stood upon them. The old creamy brown church on one side; on the other the pretty new Sunday school house; in front, at the end of the avenue of elms, the brown door of the parsonage. Matilda felt as if her own·life had got away from out of peaceful enclosures; and she walked up the avenue slowly; too slowly for such a young life-traveller. She had no need to knock this time, but just opened the door and went straight to Mr. Richmond's study.

That was peace itself. It was almost too pleasant, to Matilda's fancy. A cool matting was on the floor; the light softened by green hanging blinds; the soft gloom of books, as usual, all about; Mr. Richmond's table and work materials and empty chair telling of his habitual occupation; and on his table a jar of beautiful flowers, which some parishioner's careful hand had brought for his pleasure. The room was sweet with geranium and lily odours; and so still and pure-breathed, that the flowers in their depth of colour and wealth of fragrance seemed to speak through the stillness.   Matilda did not ask what they said, though maybe she heard. She came a little way into the room, stood still and looked about her a while; and then the child flung herself down on her knees beside a chair and burst into a passion of weeping.

It lasted so long and was so violent that she never heard Mr. Richmond come in. And he on his part was astonished. At the first sound of his voice Matilda stopped crying and let him raise her from the floor; but he did not put her into a chair. Instead of that he sat down himself and drew her to his side. Of course he asked what the matter was. Also of course Matilda could not tell him. Mr. Richmond found that out, and then took another road to his object. He let Matilda get quite quiet; gave her a bunch of grapes to eat, while he seemed to busy himself among his books and papers; at last put that down and took Matilda's plate from her.

" You do not come to church in the evening lately, I observe, Tilly," he remarked.

" No, sir.   Aunt Candy does not like me to go."

" And you have not been to the prayer meeting either, or to the meetings of our Commission.   The 'Band' is called our 'Christian Commission,' now."

" No, sir."   And Matilda's eyes watered.

" For the same reason ? "

" Yes, sir."

" Not because you have lost pleasure in such meetings ? "

" O no, Mr. Richmond!   Did you think I had ? " she asked timidly.

" I could not *know*, you know," said Mr. Richmond, " and I wanted to ask you.   I am very glad to hear it is no bad reason that keeps you away."

" I didn't say *that*, Mr. Richmond," Matilda answered slowly.   " Could it be a good reason ? "

" Why it might," said Mr. Richmond cheerfully. "You might be not well enough; or you might have more important duties to do at home; or you might be unwilling to come alone; and all those might be good reasons for staying away."

"It was no such reason," said Matilda.

There was silence.

"You wanted to talk to me, you said," Mr. Richmond observed.

"Yes, Mr. Richmond, I do; if I only knew how."

"Is it so difficult? It never used to be very difficult, Matilda."

"No, sir; but things are — different."

"*You* are not different, are you?"

"I don't know" — said Matilda slowly; — "I am afraid so. I feel very different."

"In what way?"

"Mr. Richmond," she went on, still slowly, and as if she were meditating her words, — "I don't see how I can do just right."

"In what respect?" said the minister very quietly. Again Matilda paused.

" Mr. Richmond — is it always wrong to hate people ? "

" What things should make it right for us to hate people ? "

" I don't know " — said Matilda in the same considering way ; — " when there isn't the least thing you can love them for, or like them ? "

" What if the Lord had gone by that rule in dealing with us ? "

" O, but he is so good."

" And has commanded us to be just as good, has he not ? "

" But can we, Mr. Richmond ? "

" What do you think, Tilly, the Lord meant when he gave us the order ? "

" He meant we should try."

" Do you think he meant that we should only *try*? do you think he did not mean that we should be as he said ? "

" And love hateful people ? "

" What do you think, Tilly ? "

" O Mr. Richmond, I think I'm not good."

"What is the matter, my dear child?" Mr. Richmond said tenderly, as Matilda burst into quiet tears again. "What troubles you?"

"*That,* Mr. Richmond. I'm afraid I am not good, for I am not like that; and I don't see how I can be."

"What is the hindrance? or the difficulty?"

"Because, Mr. Richmond, I am afraid I hate my aunt Candy."

Mr. Richmond was quite silent, and Matilda sobbed awhile.

"Do I understand you aright?" he said at last. "Do you say that you hate your aunt?"

"I am afraid I do."

"Why should you hate her? Is she not very kind to you?"

"I do not call her kind," said Matilda.

"In what respect is she not kind?"

The child sobbed again, with the unspoken difficulty; stifled sobs.

"She is not cruel to you?" said Mr. Richmond.

"I think she is cruel," said Matilda; "for she does not in the least care about doing things that I do not like; she does not care at all whether I like them or not. I think she likes it."

"What?"

"Just to do things that I can't bear, Mr. Richmond; and she knows I can't bear them."

"What is her reason for doing these things?"

"I think the greatest reason is because she knows I can't bear them. I think I am growing wicked."

"Is it because you displease her in any way, that she does it for a punishment?"

"I do not displease her in any way," said poor Matilda.

"And yet she likes to grieve you?"

"She said I wanted putting down. And now, I suppose I am put down. I am just in prison. I can't do anything. I can't go to Mrs. Laval's house any more. I must not go to Lilac lane any more. She won't let me. And oh, Mr. Richmond, we were going to do such nice things!" .

"Who were going to do such nice things?"

"Norton Laval and I."

"What things were they?"

"We were going to do *such* nice things! Mrs. Laval gave me money for them, and Norton, he has money always; and we were going to have Mrs. Eldridge's house cleaned, and get a bedstead, and towels, and a table, and ever so many things for her, to make her comfortable; and I thought it would be so pleasant to get the things and take them to her. And aunt Candy says I am not to go again."

"Did you tell your aunt what you were going to do?"

"O no, sir; she thinks I have no business with such things; and she does not like anybody to go into very poor houses."

"Then you did not ask her leave?"

"It never is any use to ask her anything.

She won't let me go out to church now, except in the morning, and then sometimes she makes me go with her."

Mr. Richmond was silent for some time. Matilda grew quiet, and they both were still.

"And the worst of it all is," resumed Matilda, at last, "that it makes me hate her."

"I do not like to hear you say that."

"No, Mr. Richmond,"—said Matilda very sorrowfully.

"Do you think it is right?"

"No, sir."

"Do you think you cannot help doing what is wrong."

"I don't think I can like aunt Candy."

"We will pass that. But between not liking and hating, there is a wide distance. Are you obliged to hate her?"

Matilda did not answer.

"Do you think anybody can be a child of God and have *hatred* in his heart?"

"How can I help it, Mr. Richmond?" said Matilda piteously.

"How can you help anything? The best way is to be so full of love to Jesus that you love everybody for his sake."

"But people that are not good" — said Matilda.

"It is easy to love people that are good. The wonder of the love of the Lord Jesus is, that it comes to people who are not good. And his children are like him. 'Be ye followers of God,' he tells them, 'as dear children; and walk in love.'"

"I am not like that, Mr. Richmond," Matilda said sadly.

"Didn't you love little Lem Dow? I am sure he is not very good."

"But he never troubled me, much," said Matilda. "He does not make me miserable all the day long."

Mr. Richmond paused again.

"Our Master knew what it was to be ill treated by bad people, Matilda."

"Yes, Mr. Richmond."

"How did he feel towards them?"

"O but I am not like that," said Matilda again.

"You must be, if you are his child."

"Must I?" said Matilda, the tears dropping from her eyes quietly. "How can I? If you only knew, Mr. Richmond!"

"No matter; the Lord knows. Tell him all about it; and pray to be made so like him and to love him so well, that you may love even this unkind friend."

"I don't think she is my friend," said Matilda; "but it don't make any difference."

"No, it does not make any difference."

"Mr. Richmond," said Matilda timidly after a moment, "won't you pray with me?"

Which the minister instantly did. Matilda wept quietly all the time of his prayer and after they rose from their knees, leaning her head on Mr. Richmond's shoulder where she had poured out her troubles once before. Her friend let her alone, keeping his arm round her kindly, till the child raised her head and wiped her eyes.

"Do you feel better?" he whispered then. Matilda answered "yes," in an answering whisper.

"But Mr. Richmond," she said presently, "I am very sorry for Lilac lane."

"I am very sorry," he said.

"There is the money in my purse, all ready, and our list of things. It would have been so pleasant."

"Very pleasant," Mr. Richmond answered.

"And now I can't do Band work any more," Matilda went on. "I have no opportunities for anything any more. I cannot do anything at all."

"There might be something to say about that," Mr. Richmond replied; "but I think you have had enough talk just now. Is your sorrow on account of Lilac lane because *you* have lost the pleasure? or because Mrs. Eldridge has lost it?"

"Why, both," said Matilda.

"I suppose so. Would it be any comfort

to you to know that the work was done, even though you did not see it?"

"What, you mean the house cleaned and the things got, and Mrs. Eldridge fixed up as we meant to do it?"

"I mean that."

"O yes," said Matilda. "If I could know it was done, I would not be half so sorry about it. But Norton can't manage alone; and Maria has no time."

"No, but somebody else might. Now go off and talk to Miss Redwood; and make some more gingerbread or something; and after tea we will see about your lost opportunities if you like."

"Would Miss Redwood do all that for me?" said Matilda.

"You can consult her and find out."

CHAPTER VII.

MISS REDWOOD was mopping up the yellow painted floor of her kitchen, as Matilda softly pushed open the door and looked in.

"Who's that?" said the housekeeper. "Floor's all wet; and I don't want no company till there's a place for 'em to be. Stop! is that Tilly Englefield? Why I declare it is! Come right in, child. You're the greatest stranger in town."

"But I am afraid to come in, Miss Redwood."

"Then you're easy scared. Come in, child. Step up on that cheer and sit down on my table. There! now I can look at you, and you can look at me, if you want to. I'll be through directly, and it won't take this paint no time to dry. How's all the folks at your house?"

"Gone to New York for the day; aunt Candy and cousin Clarissa are."

"Wouldn't ha' hurted 'em to have took you along. Why didn't they?"

"O they were going shopping," said Matilda.

"Well, had you any objections to go shopping?" said the housekeeper, sitting back on her feet and wringing her cloth, as she looked at Matilda perched up on the table.

"I hadn't any shopping to do, you know," said Matilda.

"I hain't no shopping to do, nother," said Miss Redwood resuming her work vigorously; "but I always like to see other folks' goins on. It's a play to me, jest to go in 'long o' somebody else and see 'em pull down all the things, and turn over all the colours in the rainbow, and suit themselves with purchases I wouldn't look at, and leave *my* gowns and shawls high and dry on the shelf. And when

I go out, I have bought as many dresses as they have, and I have kept my money for all."

" But sometimes people buy what you would like too, Miss Redwood, don't they ? "

" Well, child, not often; 'cause, you see, folks's minds is sot on different things; and somehow, folks's gowns have a way o' comin' out o' their hearts. I kin tell, pretty well, what sort o' disposition there is inside of a dress, or under a bonnet, without askin' nobody to give me a character. What's become o' you all these days? Ha' you made any more gingerbread ? "

" No."

" I guess you've forgotten all about it, then. What's the reason, ch ? "

" I have been too busy, Miss Redwood."

" Goin' to school again ? "

" No, I've been busy at home."

" But makin' gingerbread is play, child; *that* ain't work."

Matilda was silent; and the housekeeper presently came to a pause again; sat back on her feet, wrung her mopping cloth, and considered Matilda.

"Don't you want to make some this afternoon?"

"If you please; yes, I should like it," said the little girl.

"Humph!" said the housekeeper. "What have you been tiring yourself with to-day?"

"I am not tired," said Matilda. "Thank you, Miss Redwood."

"If I was to get a good bowl o' sour cream now, and shew you how to toss up a shortcake — how would you like that?"

"O I would like it very much — if I could."

"Sit still then," said the housekeeper, "till my floor's dry. Why hain't you been to see me before, eh? Everybody else in creation has been in at the parsonage door but you. You ain't beginnin' to take up with that French minister, air you?"

"O no indeed, Miss Redwood! But he isn't a French minister."

" I don't care what he is," said the house-keeper; " he takes airs; and a minister as takes airs had better be French, I think. What do you go to hear him for, then ? "

" Aunt Candy takes me."

" Then you don't go because you want to? that's what I am drivin' at."

" O no, indeed I don't, Miss Redwood. I would never go, if I could help myself."

" What harm would happen to you if you didn't? " asked the housekeeper dryly. But Matilda was distressed and could not tell.

" There is ministers as takes airs," continued the housekeeper, sitting up and giving her mop a final wring, — " but they can't kind o' help it; it's born with 'em, you may say; it's their natur. It's a pity, but so it is. That's one thing. I'm sorry for 'em, for I think they must have a great load to carry. But when a man goes to bowin' and curchying, outside o' society, and having a tailor of his own to make his coat unlike all other folks, I think I don't want to have him learn *me* manners.

Folks always takes after their minister —
more or less."

" Do you think so ? " said Matilda
dubiously.

" Why yes, child. I said *more* or *less ;* with
some of 'em it's a good deal less. Don't you
do what Mr. Richmond tells you ? "

" I try," said Matilda.

" So I try," said Miss Redwood getting
upon her feet. " La ! we all do — a little.
It's natur. Don't your aunt, now, take after
her minister ? "

" I suppose so," said Matilda with a
sigh.

" Don't you go gettin' into that French-
man's ways. Mr. Richmond's thumb is worth
all there is o' *him.*"

" Miss Redwood," said Matilda, " I want to
ask you something."

" Well, why don't you ? "

" I want to know if you won't do something for me."

" Talk away," said the housekeeper. " I

hear." She went meanwhile. getting out the flour and things wanted for the shortcake.

" There's a poor old woman that lives in Lilac lane; Mrs. Eldridge, her name is."

" Sally Eldridge," said Miss Redwood. " La! I know her. She's poor, as you say."

" You know where she lives ? "

" Course I do, child. I know where everybody lives."

" You know she is very poor; and her house wants cleaning; and she hasn't a great many things to be comfortable."

" How come *you* to know it? " asked the housekeeper.

" I have been there. I have seen her. I know her very well."

" Who took you there ? "

" Nobody took me there. I heard about her, and I went to see her."

" You didn't learn that of the French minister."

" But he is not French, Miss Redwood."

" I wisht he was," said the housekeeper.

"I say nothin' agin other country people, only to be sorry for 'em; but I get put out o' my patience when I see one of the right stock makin' a fool of himself. Well honey, what about Mis' Eldridge?"

"I've got some money, Miss Redwood, — somebody gave me some money, to get things for her and do what I like; and Norton Laval and I were going to have her made nice and comfortable. But now aunt Candy will not let me go there any more, and I can't do what I wanted to do; and I thought — Mr. Richmond thought — maybe you would see to it for me."

"What's to be done?" said the housekeeper.

"Why, first of all, Miss Redwood, her house wants cleaning. It is not fit to put anything nice into it."

"All Lilac lane wouldn't be the worse of a cleanin'," said the housekeeper; "men and women and all; but I don't know who's to do the cleanin'."

"I thought, maybe Sabrina Rogers would do it, — if she was paid, you know. She lives just over the way, and she *is* pretty clean."

"Kin try," said the housekeeper. "No harm in tryin'. I guess a dollar would fetch her round. Supposin' it was cleaned; what's to do next?"

"Get things, Miss Redwood," said Matilda looking up at her eagerly. "You know she wants so much. I want to get a bedstead for her, and a decent bed; her bed isn't a bed, and it lies on the floor. And she has no way to wash herself; I want to send her a little washstand, and basin and pitcher, and towels; and a table for the other room; and a saucepan to cook things in; and some bread and meat and sugar and other things; for she hasn't comfortable things to eat. And one or two calico dresses, you know; she wants them so much."

The child's face grew excitedly eager. There came a glitter in the housekeeper's faded blue eye as it looked down upon her.

"But honey, all these things 'll cost a sight o' money."

"I've got money."

"It'll take all you've got."

"But I want to do what I can, Miss Redwood."

"I kind o' don't think it's right," said the housekeeper. "Why should you go a spendin' all your little savin's upon Sally Eldridge? And it's only one old woman helped, when all's done; there's lots more. It's somebody else that ought to do it; 'tain't your work, child."

"But I want to do it, Miss Redwood. And I've got the money."

"I wonder how much better she'll be at the end of six months," said the housekeeper. "Well, you want me to take this job in hand, do you?"

"If you can,—if you would be so very good."

"You make me feel as mean as water," said the housekeeper. "It'll take me a little while to get up any notion o' my goodness again. I suppose it'll come, with the old pride o' me. I know what the Bible says, but I kind o' didn't think it meant it; and I've been a makin' myself comfortable all my days, or workin' for it; and consolin' my conscience with thinkin' it was no use to help *one;* but now yours and mine would make two; and somebody else's would ha' been three. La! child, you make me ashamed o' myself."

"But Miss Redwood," said Matilda in much surprise, "you are always doing something for somebody; I don't know what you mean."

"Not this way, child," said the housekeeper. "I kind o' thought my money was my own, after I had worked for it."

"Well so it is."

"And so is your'n your'n; but it looks like as if what was your'n was the Lord's.

And to be sure, that's what the minister is always a sayin'; but I kind o' thought it was because he was the minister, and that Sarah Redwood hadn't no call to be just exactly as good as him."

And to Matilda's bewilderment, she saw the corner of Miss Redwood's apron lifted to wipe off a tear.

" Come, child, make your shortcake!" she began with fresh vigour. " There's water to wash your hands. Now we must be spry, or the minister 'll be wanting his tea, and I should feel cheap if it warn't ready. I've got my lesson, for to-day; and now you shall have your'n. I never did want many blows of the hammer to drive a nail into me. Here's an apron for you. Now sift your flour, just as you did for the ginger-bread; and we'll have it baking in no time. Shortcake must be made in five minutes or it'll be heavy; and it must bake almost as quick. Turn it up, dear, with the ends o' your fingers while I pour the cream in —

just toss it round — don't seem to take hold o'
nothing — kind o' play with it; and yet you
must manage to throw the mixin's together
somehow.   Yes, that 'll do very well; that 'll
do very well; you've got a real good hand,
light and firm.   Now bring it together, dear,
in one lump, and we 'll cut it in two pieces
and put it in the pans."

This was done satisfactorily and the pans
were slipped into the hot oven.   Matilda
washed her hands, and the housekeeper made
neat and swift preparations for tea.   Everything was so nice about her, her kitchen and
pantries were in such a state of order and
propriety, and so well supplied too; it was a
pleasure to see her go from one to the other
and bring out what she wanted.   Matilda
was allowed to take cups and plates and
sugar and butter from her hand, and found it
a most enlivening kind of amusement;
especially the placing her own plate and
knife, and seeing it there on Mr. Richmond's
tea-table.   Then came the excitement of

taking out the shortcake, which had puffed itself up and browned in the most pleasant manner; and then the minister was called out to tea. It was an odd little room, between the study and the kitchen, where they took tea; not big enough for anything but the table and a convenient passage round it. Two little windows looked out over a pleasant field, part of which was cultivated as the parsonage garden; and beyond that, to white palings and neat houses, clustering loosely in pretty village fashion. Among them, facing on the street which bordered the parsonage and church grounds at the back, Matilda could see the brown front of the Academy, where Norton Laval went to school; and trees mingled their green tops with the house roofs everywhere. The sun was going down in the bright western sky which was still beyond all this; and nothing disagreeable was within sight at all.

"What are you thinking about, Tilly, that you look so hard out of my windows?" the minister asked.

"Nothing, Mr. Richmond. At least — I was thinking, whether you knew Norton. Norton Laval."

"He comes to the Sunday school, I think. No, I do not know him very well. Do you?"

"O yes."

"Is he a nice fellow?"

"He is very nice, Mr. Richmond."

"Does he love the Bible as well as you do?"

"I don't think he knows much about it, Mr. Richmond," Matilda answered, looking wistful.

"If he is a friend of your's, cannot you help him?"

"I do try," said Matilda. "But, Mr. Richmond, you know a boy thinks he knows about things better than I do, or than any girl does."

Mr. Richmond smiled.

"Besides, I can't see him now," Matilda added. "I have no chance." · And a cloud came over her face.

"Miss Redwood," said the minister, "do you think you can manage a certain business in Lilac lane which Matilda had a mind to entrust to you? I suppose you have been consulting about it."

"Does Mr. Richmond think it'll do much good?" was the housekeeper's rejoinder.

"Do I think what will do good?"

"Gettin' a new bedstead and fixin's for Sally Eldridge."

"I don't know what 'fixin's' are, in this connection," said the minister. "I have heard of 'light bread and chicken fixings,' at the South."

"The bread and the chickens are comin' too, for all I know," said the housekeeper. "I mean sheets and coverlets and pillows, and decent things. She hain't none now."

"I should think she would sleep better," said the minister gravely.

"Had this child ought to spend her little treasures for to put that old house in order?"

It's just sheddin' peas into a basket that has got no bottom to it."

" So bad as that ? " said the minister.

" Well, Mr. Richmond knows," the housekeeper went on, " there ain't no end o' the troubles there is in the world, nor yet o' the poverty; and Sally Eldridge, she'll be the better maybe, as long as the things last; but there's all the rest o' Lilac lane, without speaking of what there is beside in Shadywalk; and the child'll be without her dollars, and the world'll be pretty much where it was."

" I don't see but that reasoning would stop my preaching, Miss Redwood."

" I don't mean it, sir, I'm sure."

" I don't think you mean what you say. What is the use of giving me a good cup of tea, when so many other people cannot have one at all ? "

" The minister knows a cup o' good tea when he sees it," answered the housekeeper.

Mr. Richmond laughed. " But don't you

think Sally Eldridge, for instance, would know a good bed?"

"There ain't no possibilities o' makin' some o' them folks keerful and thrivin'," said the housekeeper firmly. "'Tain't in 'em; and what's the use o' havin' things if folks ain't keerful? Sally Eldridge had her house respectable once; I mind her very well, when she kept the gate at Judge Brockenhurst's big place; and she had wages, and her man he had good wages; and now the peas is all out o' the basket. And is there any use, buyin' more to put in? The basket'll never be mended. It'll let out as fast as it takes in."

"The basket, as you put it, is out of Sally's hands now," Miss Redwood. "She is one of the helpless ones. Don't you think it would be a good thing to make her life more comfortable? I think we had better take her some of this shortcake, Matilda. Miss Redwood, as for you, I shall expect to hear that you have lamed your arm doing something for her comfort, or half broken your back carrying a heavy basket to Lilac lane; or something of that sort; judging by what I know of you already."

"I'm willin'," said the housekeeper. "But it ain't this child's business. She hain't no call to give all she's got to Sally Eldridge."

"I suppose," said the minister, with a look at Matilda which both she and the housekeeper read with their hearts, — "I suppose she is thinking of the word that will be spoken one day; 'Inasmuch as ye did it unto one of the least of these,' — 'He that hath pity upon the poor, lendeth to the Lord; and that which he hath given will he pay him again'!"

"Then Mr. Richmond thinks it would be a good use of her money?"

"There might possibly be better. But if it is the best she knows, that is all she can do. I have a great opinion of doing what our hands find to do, Miss Redwood; if the Lord gives other work, he will send the means too."

" There's a frame bedstead lyin' up in the loft," said the housekeeper. " 'Tain't no good to any one, and it only wants a new rope to cord it up; perhaps the minister would let Sally have that; and it would save so much."

" By all means, let her have that; and anything else we can spare. Now, Matilda, you and I will go and attend to our other business."

They went back to the study, where the light was growing soft. Mr. Richmond drew up the blinds of the west window and let in the glow and colour from a rich sunset sky. He stood looking at it, with the glow upon his face; and standing so, spoke, —

" What was it, Matilda ? "

Matilda on her part sat down in a chair and with a face of childish grave meditation, peered into the great bunch of asparagus with which Miss Redwood had filled the minister's chimney. She sat in shadow all over, and answered as if taking out the very secret burden of her heart for her friend's inspection.

" Mr. Richmond, I can't do Band work any more.   I can't do anything.   I can't do anything at all.   You told us to buy up opportunities; but I have no opportunities now even to buy."

" Are you sure ? "

" Yes, sir," said the child slowly.   " I am quite sure. I cannot do any work at all. And I would like it so much."

" Wait a bit," said the minister, still looking at the evening glow; " maybe you are too hasty."

" No, sir.   Aunt Candy will not let me go out, and I can see nobody."

" Whose servant are you ? "

" I am Christ's servant," said the child softly.

" Well.   Being his servant, do you want to do his will, or your own ? "

" Why — I want to do his will," Matilda answered, speaking a little slowly.

" Isn't it his will just now that you should be without your old liberty, and unable to do these things you want to do ? "

" Yes, sir," Matilda said rather unwillingly. " I suppose it is."

" Are you willing his will should be done ? "

Mr. Richmond had faced round from the window now, and Matilda met his look, and did not answer for a moment.

" Is it his will, Mr. Richmond, that I should have no opportunity to do anything."

" What do you think ? If he had chosen to do it, he could have placed you in the midst of the fullest opportunity. He *has* placed you under the rule of your aunt. Are you willing his will should be done, and as long as he pleases ? "

Matilda looked in her friend's face, but it put the question steadily; and she faltered and burst into tears.

" That is a great question, Tilly," said the minister kindly. "Is it yourself you want to please ? or the Lord Jesus ? He can have these outside things done by other people, even if you cannot help in them; but of *you* the first thing he wants is an obedient child.

15

Will you be obedient? That is, will you agree to his will?"

" Mr. Richmond — must I be *willing* to do nothing?" Matilda asked without uncovering her face.

" If the Lord bids you do nothing."

" But I thought — he bade me — do so many things?"

" So he does; and just now the very first and foremost of them is, that you should be content with his will."

The daylight had faded sensibly when the next words were spoken, so many seconds went by before Matilda was ready to speak them.

" Mr. Richmond," she said, after that pause of hidden struggle, — " isn't it very hard?"

" It depends upon how much any one loves the Lord, my dear child. The more you love him, the less you want your own will. But you were never more mistaken in your life, than just now, when you thought he had taken all your opportunities away."

" Why, what opportunities have I, Mr. Richmond?" said Matilda lifting up her face.

" This, for one. Opportunity to be obedient. The Bible says that Christ, coming here to stand in our place and save us, learned obedience by the things which he *suffered;* and I don't know but we must, too."

Matilda looked very hard at her adviser; it was not easy for her to get at this new thought.

" Cannot you as truly obey, when God says you must be still, as when he says you must work ? "

" Yes, sir."

" And in either case, obedience is in the heart — not in the fingers or the tongue. Isn't it so ? "

" Yes, sir."

" You see one opportunity, Matilda."

" Yes, sir." The answers were very meek.

" My dear child, is that the only one ? "

. " I cannot go out, Mr. Richmond."

"No, I understand. But in the house. Have you no opportunities to be patient, for instance?"

"Yes, sir!" and a faint colour rose in Matilda's cheek.

"My child, patience is something that when God's children shew, they always honour him."

"How, Mr. Richmond?"

"It shews his grace and power in them; for they cannot be truly patient without his help. And then others see it and acknowledge that there is reality in religion, and that God's will is beautiful."

"I never thought of that," said Matilda.

"Have you no opportunity to forgive injuries, or unkindness?"

"O yes, Mr. Richmond!" The answer came from some deep place in Matilda's heart.

"Do you use that opportunity well?"

"I don't think I have, Mr. Richmond," said Matilda, looking very sorrowful. "I think, instead, I have been hating my"—

" Yes.   Shall that be at an end now ? "

" But how can it ? " said Matilda. " I get so vexed " — And she wiped away a tear. " I get *so* vexed, Mr. Richmond ! "

" I am very sorry you have occasion. But you cannot forgive people *unless* you have occasion."

" How can I then ? "

" By going to Jesus, just as the sick people went to him in the old time; and getting cured, as they did. ' If thou canst believe ; all things are possible to him that believeth.' "

Matilda steadied her trembling little lips, and stood listening.

" Haven't you opportunities to do kind-nesses ? " Mr. Richmond then said softly. Matilda looked up and bowed her head a little. Perhaps lips were not ready.

" Do you use *them* well ? "

" I think not, Mr. Richmond — lately."

" You know, you can do kindness indoors as well as out of doors ; and to disagreeable people as well as to nice people. We are commanded to be followers of God, as dear children."

The tears gathered again.

" See how much kindness you can do. No matter whether it is deserved or not. That is no part of the question. And have you not opportunity to learn something ? "

" I am not going to school," said Matilda.

" Nor learning anything at home ? "

" Not much. Not much that is good for anything."

" Never mind. You can do that for God."

" O no, Mr. Richmond; it is not useful enough."

" You do not know how useful it may be."

" Yes, sir, because it isn't that sort of thing. Aunt Candy is making me learn to mend lace. It is no use at all."

" I'll tell you a secret," said Mr. Richmond. Matilda looked up with fresh eagerness into his face.

" Whenever the Lord puts you in the way of learning *anything,* you may be sure he means you to learn it. He knows the use; and if you neglect the chance, the next thing will be, you will find he will give you work to do which you cannot do, because you neglected to learn what he gave you to learn."

"But mending lace?" said Matilda.

"I don't care what it is. Yes, mending lace. I don't know what use you will find for that accomplishment, and you don't; all the same, you *will* know, when the time comes; and then you will be very sorry and mortified to find yourself unable for the work given you, if you despised your opportunity of preparation. And then it will be too late to mend that, as well as the lace."

" And is that true of all sorts of things, Mr. Richmond? "

" Of all sorts of things. Whenever the Lord puts a chance of learning something in your way, you may be quite sure he has a use and a meaning in it. He has given it to you to do."

"Then all my learning to cook, and do things about the house?"

"Yes," said Mr. Richmond smiling. "It is not difficult to see a use for that; is it?"

"No, sir—I suppose not," the child said thoughtfully.

"Have you not opportunities for being thankful too, in the midst of all these other things?"

"Yes, Mr. Richmond."

But the child stood looking at him with a wistful, intent face, and wide-open, thoughtful eyes; so sober and so eager and so pitiful, that it made an unconscious plea to the minister's heart.

"Come," said he; "we have so much to say to our Lord, let us say it."

And they kneeled down, and Mr. Richmond put all Matilda's heart into a prayer for her, and some of his own.

"I must go now, Mr. Richmond"—Matilda said presently after. But she said it with a much more cheerful tone.

" I shall want to hear how you get on,"
said Mr. Richmond. " When will you take
tea with me again ? "

" O I don't know, sir. Aunt Candy is
always at home."

" And keeps you there ? "

" Yes, sir. Lately. She didn't at first."

" Well, I must see about that. I think you
must be allowed to come and see me, at all
events. Perhaps you do not know, Matilda,
that your mother in almost the last hour of
her life asked me to take care of you."

" Did she ? " Matilda exclaimed, with a
wonderful change of voice and manner.

" Yes. She did. In your aunt's pres-
ence."

" And you will, Mr. Richmond ? " said the
child, a little timidly.

" And I will — while I live myself."

" Then I *can* come and see you, Mr. Richmond ? "

" I think you can. I will see about it."

Matilda gave her friend a good night which

was almost joyous; and then ran out to the kitchen.

"Miss Redwood," she said, "did you change your mind again about Mrs. Eldridge? I thought you agreed, and that you were going to do all that for me."

"No, child; I hain't changed my mind. I changed it oncet, you know, to come over to you. I never did go both ways, like a crab."

"But you said at tea "—

"Well, I wished the minister'd tell you to keep your money to hum. 'Tain't *your* work, as I can see, to fit out Sally Eldridge with notions; it's like enough it's mine, and I'm willin' to take it, and do it, and see to it. You put your money by, child, against a wet day. Maybe you'll want it yet."

"Don't you remember, Miss Redwood, what Mr. Richmond repeated at tea? — 'the Lord will pay it again?'"

"Well," said the housekeeper, "let the pay come to me, then."

"No," said Matilda, "that won't do. It's

my business, Miss Redwood, and I asked you to do it for me ; and I'll give you the money. How much do you want ? "

" I hain't bought the things yet; I don' know; and some of 'em won't have to be bought, with a little contrivance. . I'll spend the least I kin; and then we'll talk about it."

Matilda gave her an energetic kiss and hurried away. But I am afraid the house-keeper's apron went up to her eyes again.

CHAPTER VIII.

MATILDA went home with new strength, and full of the will to do the very best she could in her hard circumstances. But the next morning's dousing and scrubbing and rubbing down seemed more fierce than ever. If Matilda ever ventured to say "O don't!" — Mrs. Candy was sure to give her more of what she did not like. She had learned to keep her tongue still between her teeth. She had learned to wince and be quiet. But this morning she could hardly be quiet. "Can I help hating aunt Candy?" she thought to herself as she went downstairs. Then she found Maria full of work for which she wanted more fingers than her own; and Matilda's were very busy till breakfast time, setting the table, hulling strawberries, sweep-

ing the hall, making coffee, baking the bis-
cuit. Both the girls busy, and Maria cross.
Breakfast was not sociable; and Matilda was
summoned to go to her aunt's room as soon
as the dishes were put away.

" *Can* I help it?" thought Matilda. And
as she went up the stairs she prayed for a
loving heart, and that this feeling, which was
like a sickness, might be taken away from
her.

" What makes you look so meek?" exclaimed Clarissa, as she entered the room.
Mrs. Candy lifted her face to see.

" I like to see children look meek," she
said. " That's the way they should look.
Matilda's cold bath is doing her good."

" Mamma, you are very severe with your
cold baths!" said the young lady.

" They did *you* good once," said her
mother. " You need not speak against them.
Matilda is a different child since she has been
in my bath. Here is your lace, Matilda. I
am too busy to hear you read this morning.

Take your seat over there, and see how well you can do this; it's rather a difficult piece."

It was a very difficult piece. Matilda's heart sank when she saw it; besides that her aunt's words seemed to have taken away all the meekness she had, and to have stirred up anew all her worst feelings. She put her hand to her face to hide her eyes, while she prayed afresh for help and a sweeter spirit. She seemed to be all on edge.

"What's the matter?" said Mrs. Candy. "Begin your work, child; you'll want all the time you have got, I warn you. Don't waste your time idling."

Matilda tried to remember what Mr. Richmond had said the night before, of the uses of things; and tried to pray quietly while she was taking up threads in her lace. But remembering and praying made the tears come; and then she could not see the threads, and that would not do.

By and by she became interested in what her aunt and cousin were saying.

They were unfolding their yesterday's purchases, and talking about what they were going to do with them. Gauzes, and muslins, and other stuffs new to Matilda, were laid open on the bed and hung about over the backs of chairs, and the room looked like a mercer's shop. Here was a delicate embroidered white muslin; there a rosy gauze; there a black tissue; here something else of elegant pattern; with ribbands, and laces, and rufflings, and a great variety of pretty articles. Matilda thought her aunt and cousin were having a great deal more amusing time than she had.

"What are you doing, Matilda?" Mrs. Candy's voice said again.

"Looking at cousin Issa's things, ma'am."

"Mind your work, child. You will not have that done by dinner time."

"Why I *can't*, aunt Candy."

"You could if you had been industrious. You cannot now, very likely. But you must finish it before you leave this room."

"It is no use!" said Matilda, throwing the lace down; "I can't *near* get it done for dinner. It is very hard, and it will take a great while!"

Mrs. Candy waited a moment.

"Pick up your work," she said, "and come here and stand before me and beg my pardon."

Matilda felt as if it was impossible to do this.

"Do it, and quickly," said Mrs. Candy; "or your punishment will come to-morrow morning, child. Do not be foolish. I shall give you something hot as well as cold, I warn you."

It seemed to Matilda that she could not humble herself to do as she was bidden; and the struggle was terrible for a minute or two. It shook the child's whole nature. But the conciousness of the indignity awaiting her in case of refusal fought with the keen sense of indignity now; and conquered in time. Matilda picked up her work, came before Mrs. Candy, and asked her pardon.

" Very well," said that lady tapping her cheek carelessly; " now go and sit down and behave yourself. The lace must be finished before you leave my room."

It was a day of sharp trial to Matilda, all the more, perhaps, that it came after a time of so much relief and hope and help. Matilda was disappointed. She was not a passionate child; but for some hours a storm of passion filled her heart which she could not control. Her lace needle went in and out, keeping time to the furious swayings of indignation and resentment and mortified pride and restless despair. She was in her aunt's hands; completely in her power; helpless to change anything; obliged even to swallow her feelings and hide her displeasure. For a while that morning, Matilda felt as if she would have given almost anything for the freedom to shew her aunt what she thought of her. She dared not do it, even so much as by a look. She was forced to keep a quiet face and sit obediently mending her difficult piece of lace; and the child's heart was in great turmoil. With that, by and by, there began to mingle whispers of conscience; little whispers that anger and hatred and ill-will were not right, nor becoming her profession, nor agreeing at all with that "walking in love" which Mr. Richmond had spoken of the night before. And sorrow took its part too among the feelings that were sweeping over and through her heart; but Matilda could not manage them, nor rule herself, and she at last longed for the dinner bell to ring, when her aunt and cousin would leave her and she would be alone. Lace-mending got on very slowly; her eyes were often dim, and it hindered her; though she would not let the tears fall. When the bell rang, and the door was locked upon her, Matilda's work dropped, and she too herself almost fell upon her knees in her eagerness to seek and get help. That was what she prayed for; not that her aunt might grow kind, nor that she might be somehow separated from her and taken from her rule; but that she might have help to be right; a heart to love and bear and forgive and be gentle. Matilda prayed and prayed for that; while her lace lay on the floor, and the dinner downstairs was gloomily going on.

"What's the matter with Matilda to-day?" Maria had inquired.

"Only a little impatience of her duties," Mrs. Candy had replied quietly.

"I don't see what duties she can have, to keep her shut up in your room," said Maria hotly.

"No. My dear, there are a great many things you cannot see yet. And where you cannot see, it is rather wise not to give opinion."

"I have a right to an opinion about my sister, though," said Maria; "and she isn't getting any good with all your shutting her up."

"There I think differently from you, Maria. Matilda can darn stockings now in a way I am not ashamed of; much better than you can, I assure you; and she is going on to learn lace-mending beautifully."

" What use is that to her, I should like to know!" said Maria scornfully.

" It may be some use to me," said Mrs. Candy.

" You are doing Matilda a great deal of mischief," said Maria. " She is not the same child she was."

" No, she is not," said Clarissa. " She is a great deal better behaved."

" Yes. I have taught her to know her place," said Mrs. Candy. "It is a pity that is what *you* never were taught, Maria. You are too old now. I couldn't take a switch to you, and that's the only way."

" You never did to her?" exclaimed Maria, blazing with fury.

" I never did," said Mrs. Candy. " But Matilda knows I would, at a moment's notice, if necessity came. I may do it yet, but I rather think I shall have no occasion."

" You are a horrid woman!" exclaimed

Maria. " *Of use to you.* Yes, that is just what you care about. You want Matilda for a little drudge, to mend your stockings, I suppose, and darn your lace. You are too mean to live. If mamma had only known " —

When people get so far as this in a burst of helpless rage, the next thing usually is tears; and Maria broke down accordingly. Mrs. Candy and Clarissa finished their dinner and went away.

" One cannot stand much of this sort of thing, mamma," said Clarissa as they mounted the stairs.

" I am not going to stand much of it," replied Mrs. Candy. " I am rather glad of this outburst. It gives me the opportunity I wanted."

" What will you do, mamma ? "

" I have been thinking for some time what I would do. This just gives me the opening. I will get rid of this girl."

" And what will you do with her ? "

" Let her go learn her sisters' trade; or

some other, if she likes.   We do not suit each other, and I am tired of it."

" Yes, and mamma, though it is so good of you to keep her in this way, do you know you get no thanks for it ? "

" O I never looked for thanks," said Mrs. Candy.

. " No, but I mean, people do not give you credit for it, mamma.   I know they do not."

" Like enough.   Well — I won't ask them."

" And you will keep the little one ? "

" She's manageable.   Yes, I will keep her. I like the child.   She's pretty, and clever too; and she'll be very nice when she grows up. I'll keep her.   I shall want her some day, when you get married."

" Besides, I suppose people would say ill-natured things if you did not keep one of them," said Clarissa.   " Matilda has a temper; but she minds you, mamma."

" I have got her in hand pretty well," said Mrs. Candy as she unlocked the door.   "Well, is that lace done ?   Not ?   Let me see.   You have not done a dozen stitches while I have been away!"

"I'll do it now," said Matilda; so quietly and with a voice so cleared of all roughness or ill-temper, that Mrs. Candy after looking at her, passed on to her seat and said nothing further.

But it cost Matilda some hours yet of patient diligence, before her task was ended. Then she brought it to her aunt for approval. No fault was found with it, and she was free to go downstairs to Maria. Maria had got out of the weeping mood·into dry fury again.

"I am not going to stand it!" she said.

"What are you not going to stand?"

"This way of going on. I will not put up with it any longer."

"What can you do, Maria?"

"I'll go away. I will! I declare I will. I will not be aunt Candy's cook and waiter any longer. I am not going to stand it. She may get her own dinners — or get a girl."

"But where can we go, Maria? It is no use to talk so. We haven't any place."

"She may keep you," said Maria; "but I'll go. I can't stand it. I don't know where. Somewhere! Anywhere would be better than this."

"I couldn't live here without you, Maria, you know," said the little one. "Don't talk so. What has made you angry to-day?"

"Why, the way you are served; and the way I am talked to."

"Me?" said Matilda. "Never mind. You and I have a good deal of time to ourselves, Maria. I shall get along, and I shall not mind so much. Don't you mind."

"I won't stay and see it," said Maria stoutly; "nor I won't stay and bear my part of it."

"I quite agree with you," said Mrs. Candy, walking in from the other room. The girls were in the kitchen. "I quite agree with you, Maria. It is as unpleasant for me as it is for you, and you are doing no good to Matilda.

It will be much better for us to separate. I have been thinking so for some time. You may choose what you will do, and I will make arrangements. Either you may join Anne and Letitia in town and learn the business they are learning; or if you like any other business better, I will try and arrange it for you. Let me know to-morrow morning what you decide upon, and I will finish up the matter at once. I am quite tired of the present state of things, as you say."

Mrs. Candy finished her harangue and swept out by the other door. Nobody had interrupted her; and when she was gone nobody spoke. The two girls looked at each other, Maria with a face of consternation, Matilda white with despair. You might have heard a pin fall in the kitchen, while Mrs. Candy's footsteps sounded in the hall and going up stair after stair. Then Matilda's head went down on the table. She had no words.

" The old horrid old thing!" was Maria's

exclamation. "She came and listened in the other room!"

But Matilda did not answer, and there was no relief in the explanation.

"I won't go!" said Maria next. "I won't go, unless I'm a mind to. It's my mother's house, not hers."

Matilda had no heart to answer such vain words. She knew they were vain.

"Why don't you speak!" said Maria impatiently. "Why do you sit like that?"

"It's no use, Maria," said the little one without raising her head.

"What is no use? I said I wouldn't go; and I will not, unless I choose. She can't make me."

"She will!" said Matilda, in a burst of despairing tears.

And she did. Before the week was over, Maria was relieved at her post in the kitchen and established with a dressmaker, to learn her trade. But not in Shadywalk. Mrs. Candy thought, she said, that Maria would have a better chance in a larger town, where there was more work and a larger connection; so she arranged that she should go to Poughkeepsie. And thither Maria went, to live and learn, as her aunt remarked.

The change in Matilda's life was almost as great. She had no more now to do in the work of the house; Mrs. Candy had provided herself with a servant; and instead of cooking and washing dishes and dusting and sweeping, Matilda had studies. But she was kept as close as ever. She had now to write and cipher and study French verbs and read pages of history. Clarissa was her mistress in all these, and recitations went on under the eye of Mrs. Candy. Matilda's life was even a more busy one than it had been before. Her lessons were severe, and were required in perfection; she was forced to give many hours a day to the preparing of them; and these hours were always in the afternoon and evening. The mornings were spent still in Mrs. Candy's room. When the art of darning lace was mastered, her aunt decided that it was good for her to learn all kinds of sewing. Clarissa and her mother were engaged in making up a quantity of dresses out of the materials they had purchased in New York; and Matilda was set to run up breadths of skirts, till she could do that thoroughly; then she was made to cover cord, by the scores of yards, and to hem ruffles, and to gather them, and to sew on bindings, and then to sew on hooks and eyes; and then to make button-holes. The child's whole morning now was spent in the needle part of mantua-making. After dinner came arithmetic and French exercises and reading history; and the evening was the time for reciting. Matilda was too tired when she went up to bed to do more than look at a verse or two in her Bible and make a very short prayer; she almost dropped asleep while she was doing that. However, in the morning she had a little time now, not having to go down to get breakfast; but the long lessons

before her were a sore temptation to cut
short her Bible reading. Nevertheless Matilda would not cut it short. It was the
child's one happy time in all the day. The
rest was very heavy, except only as the sweetness of Bible words and thoughts abode with
her and came up to her, bringing comfort and
giving energy. She was trying with all her
might to buy up her opportunities. She
studied her lessons as if that were the only
thing in the world to do ; and in the hours of
sewing, Mrs. Candy found her a most excellent help; quick, and neat, and skilful, and
very apt to learn. Matilda was learning fast
many things; but the most precious of all
were, to be silent, to be patient, to be kind, and
to do everything with an endeavour to please
God in it. Her little face grew pale with
confinement and steady work; it grew fine
also with love and truth. It grew gentle with
the habit of gentleness, and sweet with the
habit of forgiving. But all the while it grew
pale. She was very lonely and unspeakably

sad, for such a child. Her aunt kept her too close; gave her no liberty at all; even on Sundays she had put a stop to the little Bible readings in the Sunday school, by not letting Matilda go till the regular school time. She never went to Lilac lane; never to Mrs. Laval's. She did go sometimes to the parsonage; for Mr. Richmond had managed it; Matilda did not know how; and once she had met Norton in the street and told him how things were with her, at which he was intensly and very gratifyingly displeased. But his displeasure could not help. The weeks went steadily on with a slow grinding power, as it felt to Matilda. There seemed to be less and less of her every week, to judge by her own sensations. Less spirit and spring; less hope and desire; less strength and pleasure. Work was grinding her down, she thought; work and discipline. She was getting to be a little machine that her aunt managed at pleasure; and it did not seem to herself that it was really Matilda Englefield

any longer. She was a different somebody.
And that was in a measure true. Yet the
work doing was more and better than she
knew. It was not all lace-mending and
mantua-making and learning rules of arithmetic and French verbs. The child was
growing pale, it is true; she was also growing strong-hearted in a new way. Not in
the way of passion, which is not strong;
but in the way of patience. Self command
was making her worth twice as much as she
ever had been in her life before. Matilda
constantly did what she would rather not, and
did it well. She sewed when she would have
liked to do something else; she studied when
she was tired; she obeyed commands that
were hateful to her; she endured from her
aunt what her child's heart regarded as un-
speakable indignities and disagreeablenesses;
and she bore them, she was forced to bear
them, without a murmur; without a sign of
what she felt. More than that. Since her
last recorded talk with Mr. Richmond Matilda

had been striving to bear and to do without anger or impatience; she had prayed a great deal about it; and now it was getting to be a matter of course to oppose gentleness and a meek heart to all the trials that came upon her. In proportion as this was true, they grew easier to bear; far less hard and heavy; the sting seemed to be going out of them. Nevertheless the struggle and the sorrow and the confinement made the child's face grow thin and pale. Mrs. Candy said it was the hot weather.

July and August passed in this manner; and then September. This last month was the hardest of all; for Mr. Richmond was away from Shadywalk, on some business which kept him nearly all the month.

Towards the end of it, Matilda coming back one afternoon from doing an errand, was met suddenly near the corner by Norton Laval.

"Matilda!" he exclaimed seizing both her hands. "Now I have got you. Where have you been?"

" Nowhere."

" What have you been doing ? "

" A great many things, Norton."

" I should think you had! Why haven't you been to see mamma? She has wanted to see you. Come now."

" O no, I can't, Norton! I can't. I must go right home."

" Come after you have gone home."

" I cannot, Norton."

" Why not ? "

" I can't get leave " — Matilda whispered.

" Leave ? " said Norton. " Whose leave can't you get? That " —

" O never mind, Norton; I can't. I would come if I could." And Matilda's eyes bore witness.

" Who hinders ? " said Norton.

" Aunt Candy. Hush! don't tell I said so."

" Don't tell ! " said Norton in a very in-censed tone; " why, are you afraid of her ? "

"I mustn't stop, Norton. I must go home."

"Are you *afraid* of anybody, Pink?" he said holding her fast. "Is that why you can't get out?"

Matilda's face changed, and her lip quivered, and she did not answer.

"And what has made you grow so thin? What ails you?" pursued the boy impetuously. "You are thin and blue."

"I don't know," said Matilda. "Aunt Candy says it is the hot weather. O Norton, dear, don't keep me!"

"What have you got there?"

"Something aunt Candy sent me to buy."

"Why didn't she send a cart to fetch it?" said the boy, taking the bundle out of Matilda's hand. "Where have you been after this?"

"To Mr. Chester's."

"Why didn't you tell Chester to send it home? He sends mamma's things. He'd have sent it."

"I couldn't, Norton. Aunt Candy told me to bring it myself."

"What sort of a person is she? your aunt, who keeps you so close? She ain't much count, is she?"

"O hush, Norton!" said Matilda. "Don't; somebody will hear you."

"Do you like her?"

"I do not like to talk about her, Norton."

"Is she good to you?"

"Don't ask me, Norton, please. Now we are almost there; please let me have the bundle. I don't want you to come to the house."

Matilda looked so earnest, Norton gave her bundle up without another word and stood looking after her till she had got into the house. Then he turned and went straight to his mother and told her the whole story; all he knew and all he didn't know.

The end of which was, that the next day Mrs. Laval called to see Mrs. Candy.

Now this was particularly what Mrs. Candy had wished to bring about, and did not know how. She went to the parlour with secret exultation, and an anxious care to make the visit worth all it could be. No doubt Mrs. Laval had become convinced by what she had seen and heard, that Mrs. Candy and her daughter were not just like everybody else, and concluded them to be fit persons for her acquaintance. But yet the two confronted each other on unequal ground. Mrs. Candy was handsomely dressed, no doubt; from her cap to her shoe, everything had cost money enough; "why can't I throw it on like that?" was her uneasy mental reflection the minute after she was seated. She felt as if it clung about her like armour; while her visiter's silks and laces fell about her as carelessly as a butterfly's wings; as if they were part of herself indeed. And her speech, when she spoke, it had the same easy grace — or the carelessness of power; was it that? thought Mrs. Candy.

She had come to ask a favour, Mrs. Laval

said. Mrs. Candy had a little niece, whom her boy Norton had become very fond of. Mrs. Laval had come to beg for the possession of this little niece as long at least as a good long visit might be made to extend.

"Three or four days, for instance?" said Mrs. Candy.

"O no! that would be nothing. Three or four weeks."

She is very much at her ease! thought Mrs. Candy. Shall I let her have her will?

Mrs. Candy was in a quandary. She did not like to refuse; she coveted Mrs. Laval's notice; and this visit of Matilda's might be the means, perhaps, of securing it. Then also she and her daughter had in contemplation a journey to Philadelphia and a visit there for their own part; and it had been a question what they should do with Matilda. To take her along would make necessary a good deal of fitting up, as a preliminary; Matilda's wardrobe being in no readiness for such a journey. Truth to tell, it was not very proper for a visit to Mrs. Laval either; but Mrs. Candy reflected that it would cost much less on the whole to leave her than to take her, and be really very much a saving of trouble. Any loss of discipline, she remembered, could be quickly made up; and the conclusion of the whole was that she accepted Mrs. Laval's invitation, with no more than a few minutes of hesitation during which all these thoughts passed through her mind.

"Thank you," said that lady. "May I have her to-morrow?"

"To-morrow. Hm"— said Mrs. Candy. "I am afraid not to-morrow. I should wish to make a little preparation before the child goes to make such a visit. She has been nowhere but at home this summer."

"Let me beg that you will not wait for any such matter," said Mrs. Laval. "Send her to me just as she is. I have particular reasons for liking her to come to me immediately. If she needs anything, trust me to supply it. Shall she come to-morrow?"

You *do* take a good deal for granted very easily! thought Mrs. Candy. Then aloud,

" I should like to fit her up a little first. The child has not been away from home, and in mourning " —

" Won't you trust me to see that she does not want for anything? I assure you, I will not neglect my charge."

" You are very kind " — said Mrs. Candy; while she thought in her heart, You are very presuming!

" Then you will indulge me? " said Mrs. Laval graciously.

" If it must be so " — said Mrs. Candy, doubtful.

" Thank you! " said her visiter. " My errand is my excuse for troubling you this morning — and so early! "

Mrs. Candy felt a twinge. She had not thought it was early; she had not thought about it.

" Your place is looking beautiful," she said

as her visiter rose. "It is the prettiest place in Shadywalk."

"O I am not in Shadywalk," said Mrs. Laval. "I am on the Millbrook. Yes, it is pretty; but it is terribly hard to get servants. They won't come from New York, and there are none here."

"Not many good ones," Mrs. Candy assented.

"None that will do for me. I am in despair. I have engaged a Swiss family at last. I expect them to arrive very soon."

"From New York?"

"In New York. They are coming to me from Vevay. Father, mother, and two daughters; and I believe a boy too. They will know nothing, except farmwork, when they come; but they do make excellent servants, and so trustworthy."

"Will you want so many?"

"I will find use for them. To-morrow then. Thank you. Good morning."

Mrs. Candy stood, looking after her visiter. .

She was so elegantly dressed, and her veil was of such rich lace. She must want a goodly number of women in her household, Mrs. Candy allowed to herself, if she often indulged in dresses of fine muslin ruffled like that. And Mrs. Candy sighed. One must have money for those things, she reflected; and not a good deal of money, but a great deal. A good deal would not do. Mrs. Candy sighed again and went in, thinking that Matilda's not going this journey with her would save her quite a pretty penny. Matilda as yet knew nothing of what had been in her aunt's mind, respecting Philadelphia or Mrs. Laval either. It had all the force of a surprise when Mrs. Candy called her and told her to pack up her clothes for leaving home.

" All my clothes, aunt Erminia ? "

" You will want them all. Issa and I are going on a journey that will take us a little while — and I am going to leave you in somebody's care here; so put out whatever you will want for a couple of weeks."

Matilda wanted to ask with whom she was to be left? but that would come in time! It would be somebody not her aunt, at any rate; and she went to her room and began laying out her clothes with fingers that trembled with delight. Presently Mrs. Candy came in. She sat down and surveyed Matilda's preparations. On one chair there was a neat little pile of underclothes; on two others were similar neat little piles of frocks; some things beside were spread over the bed.

"Those are all the dresses you have got, eh?" she said.

"That's all, aunt Candy. Here are my calicoes for every day; and those are the rest; my blue spot, and my black gingham and my white. They are all clean."

"Yes," said Mrs. Candy. "Well — I guess you don't want to take these calicoes; they are pretty well worn, and you haven't any work to do now-a-days. The others won't be too nice to wear, till I come home."

"Every day?" asked Matilda.

"Yes, every day. There are not quite enough; but you must be careful and not soil them, and so make them do. There is not time to make any now, or I would get you one or two. I meant to do it."

" When are you going, aunt Candy?"

" *You* are going to-morrow. So make haste, and pack up everything you want, Matilda. I do not know whether you can do with those three frocks?"

" O yes, I will keep them clean," said the child, in her joy.

" Well I believe you can," said Mrs. Candy. " Now make haste, Matilda."

It was such glad work. Matilda made haste in her eagerness, and then pulled out things and packed them over again because it was not well done the first time. Where was she going, she wondered? Mr. Richmond was away from home still, or she should have heard more about it. Meanwhile her clothes went into the little trunk her aunt had made over to her; and her Bible was packed in a secure corner; her best boots were wrapped up and put in; and her brush and comb. Then Matilda remembered she would want these yet, and took them out again. She hesitated over her book of French verbs and her arithmetic, but finally stuck them into the trunk. It was not near full when all was done; but Matilda's heart had not a bit of spare room in it.

CHAPTER IX.

THE next day rose very bright and fair. Matilda had been sadly afraid it would rain; but no such matter; the sun looked and smiled over the world as if slyly wishing her joy on her good prospects. Matilda took it so, and got ready for breakfast with a heart leaping with delight. She had got no more news yet as to where she was going; but after breakfast Mrs. Candy made her dress herself in the gingham and put on her best boots, which made the little trunk all the emptier; and the trunk itself was locked. Things were in this state, and Matilda mending lace in her aunt's room; when Mrs. Candy's maid of all work put her head in.

"The carriage has come, mum," she said.

"What carriage?" said Mrs. Candy.

"Meself doesn't know, then. The bi says he's come fur to get the chilt."

"What boy?" said Mrs. Candy in growing astonishment.

"Sure, an' I haven't been here long enough fur to know all the bi's of the village. He's the bi that come wid the carriage, anyhow, an' it's the chilt he's wanting. An' it's the iligantest carriage you ever see in your life; and two iligant grey horses, an' a driver."

Mother and daughter looked at each other. The lace had fallen from Matilda's hands to the ground.

"Did he give no name?"

"It's just what he didn't, then. Only he jumped down and axed was the chilt ready. I tould him sure I didn't know, and he said would I go see. An' what'll I say to him, thin? for he's waitin'."

"I'll speak to him myself," said Mrs. Candy. "Go on with your work, Matilda."

But in a few minutes she came back and bade the trembling child put up her lace and 'put on her hat, and go. I am afraid the leave-taking was a short affair; for two minutes had hardly passed when Matilda stood in the hall and Norton caught her by both hands.

"Norton!" she cried.

"Yes, I've come for you. Come, Matilda, your trunk's in."

"Where are we going?" Matilda asked, as she let herself be led and placed in the carriage, which was a low basket phaeton.

"Where are we going!" echoed Norton. "Where is it likely we are going, with you and your trunk? Where did you mean to go to-day, Pink?"

"I don't know. I didn't know anything about it. O Norton, are we going to your house!"

"If Tom knows the road," said Norton coolly; "and I rather think the ponies do if he don't. Why Pink! do you mean to tell me you didn't know you were coming to us?"

"I didn't know a word about it."

" Nor how mamma went to ask for you ? "

" Aunt Candy didn't tell me."

" Did she tell you you were going any-where ? "

" Yes. She made me pack up my clothes, but that's all."

" Didn't you ask her ? "

Matilda shook her head. " I never do ask aunt Candy anything."

" Why ? " said Norton curiously.

" I don't like to — and she don't like to have me."

" She must be a nice woman to live with," said Norton. " You'll miss her badly, I should say. Aren't you sorry, Pink ? " he asked suddenly, taking Matilda's chin in his hand to watch the answer she would give. The answer, all smiling and blushing, con-tented Norton ; and the next instant the grey ponies swept in at the iron gate and brought them before the house door.

Matilda jumped out of the carriage with a feeling of being in an impossible dream.

But her boot felt the rough grave of the roadway; the sun was shining still and warm on the lawn and the trees; the mid-country, rich-coloured with hues of autumn, lay glittering in light; the blue hills were over against her sleeping in haze; the grey ponies were trotting off round the sweep, and had left her and Norton standing before the house. It was all real and not 'a dream; and she turned to Norton who was watching her, with another smile, so warm and glad that the boy's face grew bright to see it. And then there was Mrs. Laval, coming out on the verandah.

"My dear child!" she exclaimed, folding Matilda in her arms. "My dear child! I have had hard work to get you; but here you are."

"Mamma, she did not know she was coming," said Norton, "till I came for her."

"Not know it?" said Mrs. Laval, holding her back to look at her. "Why child, you have grown thin!"

" It's the hot weather, aunt Candy says."

" And pale!" said Mrs. Laval. " Yes, you have; pale and thin. Have you been ill?"

" No, ma'am," said Matilda; but her eyes were watering now in very gladness and tenderness.

" Not ill?" said the lady. "And yet you are changed, — I do not know how; it isn't all thinness, or paleness. What is the matter with you, dear?"

" Nothing — only I am so glad," Matilda managed to say, as Mrs. Laval's arms again came round her. The eyes of mother and son met expressively.

" I don't like to see people cry for gladness," whispered the lady. " That is being entirely too glad. Let us go and see where you are to live while you are with me. Norton, send York up with her box."

Matilda shook herself mentally, and went up stairs with Mrs. Laval. Such easy, soft-going stairs! and then the wide light corridor with its great end window; and then Mrs.

Laval went into a room which Matilda guessed was her own, and through that passed to another, smaller, but large enough still, where she paused.

"You shall be here," she said; "close by me; so that you cannot feel lonely."

"O I could not feel lonely," cried Matilda. "I have a room by myself at home."

"But not far away from other people, I suppose. Your sister is near you, is she not?"

"O Maria is gone, long ago."

"Gone? what entirely? Not out of the village?"

"She is in Poughkeepsie. I have not seen her in a great many weeks."

"Was that her own wish?"

"O no, ma'am; she was very sorry to go."

"Well, you must have been very sorry too. Now, dear, here are drawers for you; and see, here is a closet for hanging up things; and here is your washing closet with hot and cold water; the hot is the right hand one of these two faucets.   And I hope you will be happy here, darling."

She spoke very kindly ; so kindly that Matilda did not know how to answer.   I suppose her face answered for her; for Mrs. Laval, instead of presently leading 'the way down stairs again, sat down in a chair by one of the windows and drew Matilda into her arms. She took off her hat, and smoothed away the hair from her forehead, and looked in her face, with eyes that were curiously wistful and noteful of her.   And Matilda's eyes, wondering, went over the mid-country to the blue mountains, as she thought what a new friend God had given her.

" Are you well, dear ? " said the lady's voice in her ear softly.

" Quite well, ma'am."

" What has changed you so since last June ? "

" I didn't know that I was changed," Matilda said, wondering again.

" Are you happy, my love?"

The question was put very softly, and yet Matilda started and looked into Mrs. Laval's eyes to see what her thought was.

"Yes," said the lady smiling; "I asked you if you were quite happy. How is it?"

Matilda's eyes went back to the blue mountains. How much ought she to tell?

"I think — I suppose — I ought to be happy," she said at last.

"I think you always try to do what you think you ought to do; isn't that so?"

"I *try* " — said Matilda in a low voice.

"How happens it then, dear, that you do not succeed in being happy?"

"I don't know," — said Matilda. "I suppose I should, if I were quite good."

"If you were quite good. Have you so many things to make you happy?"

"I think I have."

"Tell them to me," said Mrs. Laval, pressing her cheek against Matilda's hair in caressing fashion; "it is pleasant to talk of one's pleasant things, and I should like to hear of yours. What are they, love?"

What did the lady mean? Matilda hesitated, but Mrs. Laval was quietly waiting for her to speak. She had her arms wrapped round Matilda and her face rested against her hair, and so she was waiting. It was plain that Matilda must speak. Still she waited, uncertain how to frame her words, uncertain how they would be understood; till at last the consciousness that she had waited a good while drove her to speak suddenly.

"Why ma'am," she said, "the first thing is, that I belong to the Lord Jesus Christ."

The lady paused now in her turn, and her voice when she spoke was somewhat husky.

"What is the next thing, dear?"

"Then, I know that God is my Father."

"Go on," said the lady, as Matilda was silent.

"Well—that is it," said Matilda. "I belong to the Lord Jesus; and I love him, and I know he loves me; and he takes care of me, and will take care of me; and whatever I want I ask him for, and he hears me."

" And does he give you whatever you ask for?" said the lady in a tone again changed.

" If he don't, he will give me something better," was the answer.

Maybe Mrs. Laval might have taken up the words from some lips. But the child on her lap spoke them so quietly, her face was in such a sweet rest of assurance, and one little hand rose and fell on the window-sill with such an unconscious glad endorsement of what she said, that the lady was mute.

" And this makes you happy?" she said at length.

"Sometimes it does," answered Matilda. " I think it ought always."

" But my dear little creature, is there nothing else in all the world to make you feel happy?"

Matilda's words were not ready.

" I don't know," — she said. " Sometimes I think there isn't— They're all away."

The last sentence was given with an unconscious forlornness of intonation which went to her friend's heart. She clasped Matilda close at that, and covered her with kisses.

"You won't feel so here?" she said.

But the child's answer was in pantomime. For she had clung to Mrs. Laval as the lady had clasped her; and Matilda's head nestling in her neck and softly returning a kiss or two, gave assurance enough.

"All away?" said Mrs. Laval. "Well, I think that too sometimes. You and I ought to belong to each other."

And then presently, as if she were shaking off all these serious reflections, she bade Matilda arrange her things comfortably in closet and drawers; and then when she liked, come down to her. So she went out, and the man with the little trunk came in and set it in a corner.

Matilda felt in dreamland. It was only like dreamland, to take out her things, which a few hours ago she had packed in the dismal precincts of her aunt's house, and place them in such delightful circumstances as her new quarters afforded. The drawers of her dressing-table were a marvel of beauty, being of a pale sea-green colour with rosebuds painted in the corners. Her little bedstead was of the same colour and likewise adorned; and so the chairs, and a small stand which held a glass of flowers. The floor was covered with a pretty white mat, and light muslin curtains lined with rose, hung before the windows. The spread on her bed was a snow white Marscilles quilt, Matilda knew that; and the washing closet was sumptuous in luxury, with its ample towels and its pretty cake of sweet fragrant soap. Every one of these things Matilda took note of, as she was obeying Mrs. Laval's advice, to put her things in some order before she came downstairs. And she was thinking also, what 'opportunities' she could possibly have here? There would be nothing to try her patience or her temper;

nothing disagreeable, in fact, except the thought of going away again. How could she ever bear *that?* And then it occurred to Matilda that certainly she had opportunity and occasion to give thanks; and she knelt down and did it very heartily; concluding as she rose up that she would leave the question of going away till it came nearer the time.

She went with a light heart downstairs then; how odd it was to be at home in that house, going up and down with her hat off! She passed through one or two rooms, and found Mrs. Laval at last in a group of visiters, busy talking to half a dozen at once. Matilda stole out again, wondering at the different Mrs. Laval downstairs from the one who had sat with her in her little room half an hour ago. On the verandah she met Norton. He greeted her eagerly, and drew her round the house to a shady angle where they sat down on two of the verandah chairs.

"Now what shall we do this afternoon?" said Norton. "What would you like?"

"I like everything. O I like everything!" said Matilda.

"Yes, but *this* is nothing," said Norton. "Shall we go take a long drive?"

"If Mrs. Laval goes — I should like it very much."

"If she don't go, we will," said Norton. "The roads are in good order; and the ponies want exercise. I don't believe mamma will go; for she is expecting a whole ship-load of servants, and Francis will have to go to the station for them."

"Then he will want the horses, won't he?"

"Not the ponies. He will get somebody's great farm wagon, to bring up all their goods and things. You and I will go driving, Pink."

"Will *you* drive?" asked Matilda.

"Certainly."

Matilda thought more than ever that she was in fairyland. She sat musing over her contentment, when Norton broke in again.

"You are very fond of that aunt of yours, aren't you?"

It was a point blank question. Matilda waited, and then softly said "no."

"Not?" said Norton. "That's funny. Hasn't she done everything in the world to make you love her?"

"Please, Norton," said Matilda, "I would rather not talk about her."

"Why not, Pink?" said Norton, shewing his white teeth.

"I don't enjoy it."

"Don't you?" said Norton. "That's funny again. I should think you would."

"Why?" said Matilda curiously.

"There's so much to say, that's one thing. And then she's so good to you."

"Who told you she was so good to me?"

"I can see it in your face."

Matilda sat silent, wondering what he meant.

"You can always tell," said Norton. "People can't hide things. I can see, she has been doing no end of kindnesses to you all summer long.   That has made you so fond of her."

Matilda was puzzled and sat silent, not knowing what it was best to say; and Norton watching her stealthily saw a wistful little face, tender and pure, and doubtful, that just provoked caresses.   He dropped what was in his hands and fairly took possession of Matilda, kissing the pale cheeks, as if she were his own particular plaything.   It was unlike most boys, but Norton Laval was independent and manly above most boys. Matilda was astonished.

"Drive? to be sure we will drive," said Norton as he let her go.   " We will drive all over creation."

The visiters went away just at this juncture, and the children were called in to dinner. And after dinner Norton made some of his words good.   Mrs. Laval was not going out; she gave leave to Norton to do what he pleased, and he took Matilda to drive in the basket phaeton.

"Norton"—she said as they were just setting forth.

"Well?"

"If you would just as lieve, I wish you wouldn't, please, go past aunt Candy's."

"Not go past?" said Norton. "Why, Pink?"

"If you would just as lieve, I would rather not."

Norton nodded, and they took another way. But now this was better than fairyland. Fairyland never knew such a drive, surely. The afternoon was just right, as Norton had said; there was no dust, and not too much sun; the roads were in fine order; and they bowled along as if the ponies had had nothing to do in a great while. Now it was hardly within the memory of Matilda to have seen the country around Shadywalk as she saw it this afternoon. Every house had the charm of a picture; every tree by the roadside seemed to be planted for her pleasure. The meadows and fields of stubble and patches of ploughed land, were like pieces of a new world to the long housed child. Norton told her to whom these fields belonged, which increased the effect, and gave bits of family history, as he knew it, connected with the names. These meadows belonged to such a gentleman; his acres counted so many; were good for so much; taken capital care of. Here were the fields and woods of such a one's farm; *he* kept cows and sent milk to New York. That house among the trees was the homestead of one of the old county families; the place was beautiful; Matilda would see it some day with Mrs. Laval; that little cottage by the gate was only a lodge. Matilda desired to know what a lodge was; and upon the explanation, and upon many more details correlative and co-related, went into musings of her own. But the sky was so fair and blue; the earth was so rich and sunny; the touches of sear or yellow leaves here and there on a branch gave such emphasis to the deep hues still lingering on the vegetation, the phaeton wheels rolled so smoothly; that Matilda's musings did not know very well what course to keep.

"Well what *are* you thinking of?" said Norton after a silence of some time.

"I was thinking of Lilac lane, just then."

"Lilac lane! Do you want to see it?"

"Very much, Norton," said Matilda gleefully; "but not this afternoon. I haven't been there in a great, great while."

"I should not think you would want to be ever there again. I can't see why."

"But then, what would become of the poor people?"

"They do not depend upon you," said Norton. "It is not *your* look-out."

"But — I suppose," Matilda said slowly, "I suppose, everybody depends upon somebody."

"Well?" — said Norton laughing.

"You needn't laugh, though, Norton; because, if everybody depends upon somebody, *then*, everybody has somebody depending upon him, I suppose."

" Who depends upon you ? "

" I don't know," said Matilda. " I wish I did."

" Not Mrs. Old-thing there, at any rate. And how can anybody tell, Pink ? "

" I don't know " — said Matilda; " and so it seems to me the best way would be to act as if everybody depended on you; and then you would be sure and make no mis- take."

" You would be making mistakes the whole time," said Norton. " It would be all one grand mistake."

" Ah, but it cannot be a mistake, Norton," — She stopped suddenly.

" What cannot be a mistake ? "

" It cannot be a mistake, to do anything that God has given you to do."

" How can you tell?" said Norton. " It's all like a Chinese puzzle. How can you tell which piece fits into which ? "

" But if every piece fitted, then the pattern would be all right," said Matilda.

"Yes," said Norton laughing; "but that is what I say!   How can you tell?"

"Mr. Richmond says, that whenever we have an opportunity to do anything or to learn anything, the Lord means that we should use it."

"I have a nice opportunity to turn you over on these rocks and smash the carriage to pieces; but I don't mean to do it."

"You know what I mean, Norton; nobody has an opportunity to do wrong. I mean, you know, an opportunity to do anything good."

"Well now, Pink," said Norton, drawing the reins a little and letting the ponies come to an easy walk, — "see what that would end in. As long as people have got money, they have got opportunities. I suppose that is what you mean?"

"Yes" — said Matilda. "That is part."

"Well. We might go on and help all the people in Lilac lane, mightn't we? and then we could find plenty more to help somewhere else; and we could go on, using our opportunities, till we had nothing to live upon ourselves. That is what it must come to, if you don't stop somewhere. We should have to sell the carriages and the ponies, and keep two or three servants instead of eight; and mamma would have to stop wearing what she wears now; and by and by we should want help ourselves. How would you like that? Don't you see one must stop somewhere?"

"Yes," said Matilda. "But what puzzles me is, where ought one to stop? Mr. Richmond says we ought to use all our opportunities."

"If we can," said Norton.

"But Norton, what we *can't*, is not an opportunity."

"That's a fact!" said Norton laughing. "I didn't know you were so sharp, Pink."

"I should like to ask Mr. Richmond more about it," said Matilda.

"Ask common sense!" said Norton. "Well, you don't want to go to Lilac lane to-day.   Is there anywhere you do want to go ? ”

“ No.   O yes, Norton.   I *should* like to stop and see if Mr. Richmond has got home, and to ask Miss Redwood a question.   If you would just as lieve.”

“ Where does Miss Redwood live ? ”

“ O, she is Mr. Richmond’s house-keeper.”

“ All right,” said Norton.   And then the grey ponies trotted merrily on, crossed a pretty bridge over a stream and turned their faces westward.   By and by the houses of the village began scatteringly to appear; then the road grew into a well built up street; the old cream-coloured church with its deep porch hove in sight; and the ponies turned just short of it and trotted up the lane to the parsonage door.   Norton jumped down and tied the horses, and helped Matilda out of the carriage.

“ Are you going in ? ” she asked.   But it appeared that Norton was going in.   So he pulled the iron knocker, and presently Miss Redwood came to the door.

"Yes, he's home," she said, almost before they could ask her; "but he ain't at home. I 'spect he'll take his meals now standin' or runnin' for the next six weeks. That's the way he has to pay for rest, when he gets it, which ain't often neither. It tires me, just to see him go; I'll tell him you called."

"But mayn't we come in, Miss Redwood? just for a minute?"

"La, yes, child," said the housekeeper making way for them, — "come in, both on ye. I didn't 'spose you was wantin' me; I've got out o' the way of it since the minister's been away; my callers has fell off somehow. It's odd, there don't one in twenty want to see me when I'm alone in the house, and could have time in fact to speak to 'em. That's the way things is in the world; there don't nothin' go together that's well matched, 'cept folks' horses: and they're out o' my line.

Come in, and tell me what you want to say. Where have ye come from ? ”

“ I have been having a delightful ride, Miss Redwood, ever so far; further than ever I went before.”

“ Down by Mr. James’s place and the mill, and round by Hillside,” Norton explained.

The housekeeper opened her pantry and brought out a loaf of rich gingerbread, yet warm from the oven, which she broke up and offered to the children.

“ It’s new times, I ’spect, ain’t it ? ”

“ It’s new times to have such good gingerbread,” said Norton. “ This is prime.”

“ Have you ever made it since I shewed ye ? ” Miss Redwood asked Matilda.

“ No — only once — I hadn’t time.”

“ When a child like you says she hain’t time to play, somebody has got something that don’t belong to him,” said the housekeeper.

“ O Miss Redwood, I wanted to know, what about Lilac lane ? ”

" Well, what about it ? "

" Did you do as you said you would ? you know, last time I asked you, you hadn't got the things together."

" Yes, I know," said the housekeeper. " Well, I've fixed it."

" You did all as we said we would have it ? " exclaimed Matilda eagerly.

" As you said *you* would have it. 'Twarn't much of it my doing, child. Yes; Sally Eldridge don't know herself."

" Was she pleased ? "

" Well, 'pleased' ain't to say much. I got Sabriny Rogers to clean the house first. They thought I was crazy, I do believe. ' *Clean* that 'ere old place ? ' says she.. ' Why yes,' says I; 'don't it want cleanin' ? ' ' But what on airth's the use ? ' says she. ' Well,' says I, ' I don't know; but we'll try.' So she went at it; and the first day she didn't do no more than to fling her file round, and you could see a spot where it had lighted; that's all. ' Sabriny,' says I, ' that ain't what we call cleanin' in *my* country; and if I pay you for cleanin' it's all I'll do; but I'll not pay nobody for just lookin' at it.' So next time it was a little better; and then I made her go over the missed places, and we got it real nice by the time I had done. And then Sally looked like somethin' that didn't belong there; and we began upon *her*. She was wonderful taken up with seein' Sabriny and the scrubbin' brush go round; and then she begun to cast eyes down on herself, as if she wished it could reform her. Well, I did it all in one day. I had in the bedstead, and put·it up, and had a comfortable bed fetched and laid on it; and I made it up with the new sheets. 'Who's goin' to sleep there?' says Sally Eldridge at last. 'You,' says I. '*Me?*' says she; and she cast one o' them doubtful looks down at herself; doubtful, and kind o' pitiful; and I knew she'd make no objection to whatever I'd please to do with her; and she didn't. I got her into a tub o' water, and washed her and dressed her; and while I was doin' that, the folks in the other room had put in the table and the other things, and brought the flour and cheese and that; and laid a little rag carpet on the floor; and when Sally was ready I marched her out. And she sat down and looked round her, and looked round her; and I watched to see what was comin'. And then she begun to cry."

" To cry!" Matilda echoed.

" The tears come drop, drop, down on her new calico; it fitted nice and looked real smart; and then, the first word she said was, 'I ain't a good woman.' 'I know you ain't,' says I; 'but you kin be.' So she looked round and round her at everything; and then, the next word she said was, 'The dominie kin come now.' Well! I thought that was good enough for one day; so I give her her tea and come home to my own, an ashamed woman."

" Why, Miss Redwood?"

" 'Cause I hadn't done it ages ago, dear, but it was left for you to shew me how."

" And is Mrs. Eldridge really better ? "

" Has twice as much sense as ever she shewed when she was in all that muss.   I am sure, come to think of it, I don't wonder. Things outside works in, somehow.   I believe, if I didn't keep my window panes clear, I should begin to grow deceitful — or melancholy.   And folks can't have clean hands and a dirty house."

" Thank you, Miss Redwood," said Matilda rising.

" Well, you ain't goin' now?   The minister 'll be in directly."

" I'll come another time," said Matilda. " I'm afraid Mrs. Laval would be anxious."

" La, she don't mind when her horses come home, I'll engage."

" But she might mind when *we* come home," said Matilda.   " We have been out a great while."

" Out? why, you don't never mean *you* come from Mrs. Laval's ? "

"Yes, she does," said Norton. "We've got her."

"Hm! Well I just wish you'd keep her," said the housekeeper. "She's as poor as a peascod in a drouth."

At which similitude Norton laughed all the way home.

CHAPTER X.

IT is impossible to tell how pleasant Matilda's room was to her that night. She had a beautiful white candle burning in a painted candlestick, and it shed light on the soft green furniture and the mat and the white quilt and the pictures on the walls, till it all looked more fairylandish than ever; and Matilda could hardly believe her own senses that it was. real. And when the candle was covered with its painted extinguisher, and the moonlight streamed in through the muslin curtains, it was lovelier yet. Matilda went to the window and gazed out. The fields and copses lay all crisp and bright in the cool moonbeams; and over beyond lay the blue mountains, in a misty indistinctness that was even more ensnaring than their midday beauty. And no bell of Mrs. Candy's could sound in that fairy chamber to summon Matilda to what she didn't like. She was almost too happy; only there came the thought, how she would ever bear to go away again.

That thought came in the morning too. But pleasure soon swept it away out of sight. She had a charming hour with Mrs. Laval in the greenhouse; after which they went up to Matilda's room; and Mrs. Laval made some little examination into the state of that small wardrobe which had been packed up the day before and now lay in the drawers of the green dressing-table. Following which, Mrs. Laval carried Matilda off into another room where a young woman sat sewing; and her she directed to take Matilda's measure and fit her with a dress from a piece of white cambrick which lay on the table.

"It's getting pretty cool, ma'am, for this sort of thing," said the seamstress.

"Yes, but it will be wanted, and it is all I have got in the house just now. I will get something warmer to-day or to-morrow, or whenever I go out. And Belinda, you may make a little sacque to wear with this; there is enough of that red cashmere left for it. That will do."

Two or three days saw the white frock done and the sacque. Mrs. Laval provided Matilda with pretty slippers and a black sash; and furthermore desired that she would put these things on and wear them at once. Matilda did not know herself, in such new circumstances, but obeyed, and went downstairs very happy. Norton cast an approving glance at her as she met him.

"Come here," said he stretching out his hand to her; "mamma's busy with her new people, and we will have another drive presently. Come and sit down till it is time to go."

They went on the verandah, where it was warm and yet shady; the October sun was so genial, and the winds were so still.

"So they have come?" said Matilda.

"Yes, a lot of them. Look as if they had come from the other end of creation. Pink, I think I'll cover all that bank with bulbs."

"What are bulbs?"

"You don't know much, if you *are* a brick," said Norton. "I mean, tulips and hyacinths and crocuses and ranunculuses and — well, I don't know all, but those specially. Wouldn't it be fine?"

Norton was a great gardener.

"I know tulips," said Matilda. "We have a bunch of red tulips in our garden. I think they are beautiful."

"I do not mean red tulips. Did you never see any but those?"

"No."

"Then you do not know what I mean by tulips. They are everything else except plain red; I shall not have one of those."

"Yellow?"

"Well perhaps I may have two or three yellow ones. They are pretty; — clear lem-on colour, you know; the colour of evening primroses."

" Are there blue tulips too?"

" Not that ever I heard," said Norton. " No, there are red, and yellow, and yellow striped with red, and white striped with red, and white blotched with carmine, and yellow edged with brown or purple, and a thousand sorts; but never a blue."

" That's odd, isn't it?" said Matilda. " And nobody ever heard of a blue rose."

" Perhaps they will, though," said Norton. " There are black roses, and green roses. But I don't believe either there *can* be a blue rose; it is against nature."

" But how many tulips will you have, Norton? you said *two or three* yellow ones; and there are a thousand sorts."

" Well, I will not have all the sorts," said Norton; " but I tell you what I will do. I will fill all that bank with them and hyacinths, I shall want a hundred or so."

" Do they cost much?"

" Pretty well," said Norton; "if you get the costly sorts. They are a dollar apiece, some of them. But plenty are nice for fifty cents, and thirty cents."

" Your tulip bed will cost — a great deal, Norton!"

" And that bed over there," Norton went on, pointing, "shall be your bed; and I will fill it with hyacinths for you. You shall choose what colours, Pink. They will be beautiful in May. Those shall be yours."

" O thank you! But do *they* cost much?"

" You always ask that," said Norton laughing. " Yes, some of them do. I will tell you what I will do, Pink — and then you will be easy. I will spend twenty five dollars on my tulip bed, and you shall spend twenty five dollars on your hyacinth bed; and you shall say now what sorts you will have."

" Twenty five dollars!" said Matilda. "O Norton, thank you. How nice! And I never saw a hyacinth in my life. What are they like?"

Norton was endeavouring to tell, when Mrs. Laval came upon the verandah. She came with business upon her lips, but stopped and her face changed when she saw Matilda.

" My dear child! " she said.

" Mamma," said Norton, " isn't she a brick ? "

" A brick ? " said Mrs. Laval, taking Matilda in her arms and sitting down with her. " A brick ! — this soft, sweet, fresh Delight of mine ! " And as she spoke she emphasized her words with kisses. " My darling! There is nothing rough or harsh or stiff about you — nor anything angular; nor anything coarse; and he calls you a brick ! "

" I think he means something good by it, ma'am," Matilda said laughing.

" I don't know about the angles," said Norton. " Pink has a stiff corner now and then that I haven't been able to break off yet."

" Break off! " said Mrs. Laval, sitting with her arms round Matilda. And then they all went off into a laugh together.

"I had forgotten what I was going to say," Mrs. Laval resumed. "When you are out, Norton, I wish you would stop and send the doctor here."

"What's the matter?"

"I don't know; but those poor people are in a state under the bank, and maybe the doctor could best tell what they want."

"Sick?" said Norton.

"No, not sick, but dull and spiritless. I don't know what is the matter. They are tired with their journey perhaps, and forlorn in a strange place. Maybe they would feel better if they saw the doctor. I think such people often do."

And then Norton and Matilda had another ride in the basket wagon.

On their return, Norton proposed that they should go down under the bank and see the new comers. Matilda was ready for anything. Under the bank, was the place for Mrs. Laval's farm-house and dairy house, and barns and stables; a neat little settlement it looked like.   A pretty little herd of cows had come home to be milked, and a woman in a strange costume, never before known at Shadywalk, had come out with a milking pail. To her Norton marched up, and addressed her in French; Matilda could not understand a word of it; but presently Norton went off into the farm-house.   Here, in the kitchen, they found the rest of the family.   A pleasant-faced middle-aged woman was busy with supper; a young pretty girl was helping her; and two men, travel-worn and bearing the marks of poverty, sat over the fire holding their heads.   Norton entered into conversation here again.   It was very amusing to Matilda, the play of face and interchange of lively words between him and these people, while yet she could not understand a word.   Even the men lifted up what seemed to be heavy heads to glance at the young master of the place; and the women looked at him and spoke with unbent brows and pleasant and pleased countenances.   But the elder woman had a good deal to say; and Norton looked rather thoughtful as he came out.

"What is it all, Norton?" Matilda asked. "Is all right?"

"Well, not exactly," said Norton. "Those two men are sick."

"Hasn't the doctor come yet?"

"Yes, and he says they want a few days of rest; but *I* say they are sick."

"But the doctor must know?"

"Perhaps," said Norton. "Perhaps he don't."

The people under the bank were forgotten soon, in the warm luxury of the drawing-room and the bright tea-table, and the comfort of sugared peaches. And then Matilda and Norton played chess all the evening, talking to Mrs. Laval at intervals. The tulip bed and the hyacinth bed were proposed, and approved; a trip to Poughkeepsie was arranged, to see Maria; and Norton told of Miss Redwood's doings in Lilac lane. Mrs. Laval was much amused.

" And you two children have done that!" she said.

" You gave me the money for it, ma'am," said Matilda.

" It was yours after I had given it," said the lady. " I wonder how much good *really* now, all that will amount to ? or whether it is just a flash in the pan ? That is the question that always comes to me."

Matilda looked up from the chess men, wondering what she could mean.

" It is a real good to have the house cleaned; you would never doubt that, mamma, if you had seen it," Norton remarked.

" And it is a real good that the poor woman is ready to have Mr. Richmond come to see her now," said Matilda.

" Mr. Richmond," repeated Mrs. Laval. " That's your minister. You think a great deal of Mr. Richmond, don't you, Matilda ? "

" Everybody does," said Matilda. Mrs. Laval smiled.

"I don't know him, you know. But about your doings in the lane — there is no end to that sort of work. You might keep on forever, and be no nearer the end. That is what always discourages me. There are always new old women to comfort, and fresh poor people to help. There is no end."

"But then "— said Matilda. She began timidly, and stopped.

"What then?" said Mrs. Laval smiling.

"Yes, just hear Pink, mamma," said Norton.

"What then, Matilda?" said Mrs. Laval, still looking at her as at something pleasant to the eyes.

"I was going to say," Matilda began again with a blush, 'isn't it meant that we *should* 'keep on forever'?"

"Doing good to the poor? But then one would soon have nothing to do good with. One must stop somewhere."

Clearly, one must stop somewhere. A line

must be found; inside or outside of her bed of hyacinths, Matilda wondered? She did not press her doubts, though she did not forget them; and the talk passed on to other things. Nothing could be more delightful than that evening, she thought.

The next day there was charming work to be done. Norton was to take her by the early train the morning after to go to Poughkeepsie; and Matilda was to prepare to-day a basket of fruit, and get ready some little presents to take to her sister. The day was swallowed up in these delights; and the next day, the day of the journey, was one long dream of pleasure. The ride to the station, the hour in the cars, or less than an hour; but the variety of new sights and sensations made it seem long; the view of a new place; the joyful visit to Maria, and the uncommonly jolly dinner the three had together at a good restaurant, made a time of unequalled delight. Only Maria looked gloomy, Matilda thought; even a little discomposed at so much

pleasure coming to her little sister and miss-
ing *her.* And in this feeling, Matilda feared,
Maria lost half the good of the play-day that
had come to her. However, nothing could
spoil it for the other two; and Matilda came
home in the cars towards nightfall again with
a heart full of content. Only a pang darted
through her, as they were driving home under
the stars, at the thought how many days of
her fortnight were already gone. Matilda did
not know it was to be a month.

They found Mrs. Laval in perplexity.

"I wish, Norton," she said, "that you
would go and bring the doctor here immediately. The two women are ailing now, and
the men are quite sick. I don't know what
to do. York is gone to town, you know, to
look after the interest on his bonds; and
Francis demanded permission this afternoon
to go and see his father who is dying. I
have no one to send for anything. I could
not keep Francis, and I do not believe he
would have been kept."

" Who's to look after the horses, mamma?"

" I don't know.   You must find some one,
for a day or so.   You must do that too, to-
night."

Norton went and came back, and the evening passed as gayly as ever ; York's absence
being made up by the services of the children,
which, Mrs. Laval said, were much better.
Matilda made toast at the fire, and poured
out tea ; and Norton managed the tea-kettle
and buttered the toast, and fetched and
carried generally ; and they had a merry time.
But the next morning shewed a change in the
social atmosphere.

Matilda came downstairs, as she always
did, the earliest of the family.   In the hall
she encountered the housemaid, not broom in
hand as usual, but with her bonnet and shawl
on.

" I'm going out this way, miss, ye see,
becaase it's shorter," she said with a certain
smothered mystery of tone.

" What is shorter? and where are you

going, Jane?" Matilda asked, struck by something in the girl's air.

" Och, it's no lady wouldn't expict one to stop, whin it's *that's* the matter."

" When what is the matter? what do you mean? Are you going away?"

" Faith, it's glad I be, to be off; and none too soon. I'd shew 'em the back of me head, you, dear, if it was me, goin' out at the front door. The likes o' you isn't obleeged to stop no more nor meself." This advice was given in the same mysterious undertone, and puzzled Matilda exceedingly.

" But Jane," she said, catching the woman's shawl as she would have left her, " you know York is away; and there is nobody to do things. Mrs. Laval will want you."

" She's welcome to want me," said the girl. " I didn't engage fur to serve in a hospital, and I won't do it. Me life is as good to me, sure, as her own or anybody's."

" But what shall I tell Mrs. Laval? Aren't you coming back?"

"Niver a bit, till the sickness is gone." And with that the girl would not be kept, but got away.

Matilda stood bewildered. Yes, she saw the broom and duster had been nowhere that morning. Everything was left. It was early yet. The sunbeams came slant and cool upon the white frost outside, as Jane opened the door; and so when the door was shut they stole in upon the undusted hall and rooms. Matilda softly made her way to the kitchen stairs and went down, fearing lest there might be more defaulters in the household. To her relief, she found the cook moving about preparing for some distant breakfast. But breakfast was never an early meal.

"Good morning, Mrs. Mattison," said the child. "I came down to see if there was anybody here. I met Jane just now, going out."

"I'm here yet," said Mattison. "I'll get your breakfast, before I'm off."

" Are you going too ? "

" Take my advice, and don't *you* stop," said the woman. " You ain't a fixture so you can't get away. I'd go, fust thing, if I was you."

" Why ? " said Matilda; " and what for are you all going like this? It is using Mrs. Laval very badly, I think."

" Folks must take care of their own flesh and blood," said the woman. " Wages don't pay for life, do they? I'm off, as soon as I've got the breakfast. I'll do that, and give Mrs. Laval that much chance. She ain't a bad woman."

" Is the laundry maid going too?"

" O' course. She had her warning, weeks ago, and so had I mine. Mrs. Laval sent for them furriners to fill her house with them; and now she must make the best of 'em she can. It ain't my fault if they're no use to her."

Matilda went upstairs again, pondering what was to be done. She went softly up to

Norton's door and knocked. It was not easy to rouse him; nothing stirred; and Matilda was afraid of awaking his mother, whose door was not far off. At last she opened Norton's door a bit and called to him.

"What is it?" cried Norton, as soon as the noise found a way to his brain. "Is it you, Pink? Hold on,— I'll be there in less than no time! What's to pay?"

Matilda waited, till in another minute Norton presented himself, half dressed, and with his hair all shaggy, outside his door.

"O Norton, can you be dressed very quickly?"

"Yes. What's the matter? I am going down to see to the horses. What do you want, Pink?"

"O Norton — speak softly! — everybody's going away; and I thought, maybe you would come down and help me get things in order."

"What *do* you mean, Pink?" said Norton opening his eyes at her.

"Hush! They are all going away."

"Who?"

"The servants. All of them. Jane is off, and the cook will only stay till after breakfast. The laundry woman is going too. Francis is away, you know, and York. There is no-body but you and me in the house — to stay. I don't know what has got into all their heads."

"You and me!" said Norton. "The un-conscionable fools! what are they afraid of?"

"Afraid of trouble, I suppose," said Matilda. "Afraid they will have nursing to do. I don't know what else."

"They ought to be put into the peniten-tiary!"

"Yes, but Norton, can you come down presently and help?"

"Help what?"

"Me. I want to set the table for breakfast, and I don't know where things are, you know. I am going to set the table, if you'll shew me."

"I should think you didn't know where things are! Stop — I'll be there directly."

Norton disappeared, but Matilda had no idea of stopping. She went downstairs softly again, and opened the windows, such of them as she could manage; applied to the powers below stairs for broom and duster, and went at her old work of putting rooms in order. But it seemed like play now, and here. She was almost glad the servants were going away, to give her the chance.

"Well, you *are* a brick!" was Norton's remark when he came in. "I suppose you know what it means by this time?"

"I wish you'd open those two windows for me, Norton; I can't undo the fastenings. Then perhaps you'd be a brick too?"

"I don't know," said Norton laughing. "Well — there, Pink. What now?"

"Shew me, Norton, where the things are."

"All at once, is rather too much," said Norton, as he and Matilda went into York's pantry. "All for nothing, too. Nursing!

nonsense! they wouldn't have to nurse those people. It's jealousy."

"Yes, I think they are jealous," said Matilda, "from something the cook said."

Norton stood and looked on admiringly, while Matilda found the tablecloth, and arranged cups and saucers and plates and spoons and mats, and all the belongings of the breakfast table.

"Have you got to go to the stables, Norton?"

"Yes."

"Well, won't you go and get back, then? The breakfast will be ready, you know."

"Forgot all about that," said Norton.

While he was gone, Matilda finished her arrangements; and was watching for him from the verandah when Mrs. Laval came behind her.

Of course it had become necessary to tell her the state of affairs. Mrs. Laval set down in one of the verandah chairs as soon as Matilda began to speak, and drew the child to her arms; wrapping them all round her, she sat thoughtfully caressing her, kissing her brow and cheeks and lips, and smoothing her hair, in a sort of fond reverie; so fond, that Matilda did not stir to interrupt her, while she was so thoughtful that Matilda was sure she was pondering all the while on what was best to do.

" Who set the table?"

" I did, ma'am.　Norton shewed me where things were."

"! *Ma'am*," repeated Mrs. Laval, drawing the child closer.　" Would it be very hard to call me 'mamma' — some time — when you know me better?　I can't let you go."

Matilda flushed and trembled; and then Norton came running up the bank.　He smiled at the sight of his mother, with Matilda in her arms and her face resting upon Matilda's forehead.

" What's the word down there this morning, Norton ? "

"I don't know, ma'am; I've only been to see the horses. *They* are well."

"To the stables, have you been? Then do run and change your dress, Norton."

"Yes, and breakfast's ready, Norton," Matilda called after him. She slid off Mrs. Laval's lap, and rang for it, and when it came up on the dumb waiter she did York's work, in setting it on the table, with a particular pleasure. She began to have a curious feeling of being at home in the house.

"There is but one thing for me to do," said Mrs. Laval, as they sat at breakfast. "I must go down to the city and get a new houseful of servants, to do till these are well. But I am in a great puzzle how to leave you two children. There will be nobody here; and I may very possibly be obliged to stay a night in town. It is not at all likely that I can do what I have to do, in time to take an evening train."

"I can take care of Pink, mamma.'

" Who will take care of you ? "

" I'll try " — said Matilda.

" What can *you* do, to take care of *me* ? " said Norton.

" You will want something to eat," said Matilda. " I think you will — before to-mor-- row night."

" If I do, I can get it," said Norton.

" He thinks dinner grows, like a cabbage," said Mrs. Laval; " or like a tulip, rather. His head is full of tulips. But I cannot go to-day to New York; I could not catch the train. I'll go downstairs and see these people after breakfast, and make them stay."

But when Mrs. Laval descended half an hour later to the regions of the kitchen, she found them deserted. Nobody was there. The fire, in a sullen state of half life, seemed to bear witness to the fact; the gridiron stood by the side of the hearth with bits of fish sticking to it; the saucepan which had held the eggs was still half full of water on the hob; the floor was unswept; the tray of eggs stood on one table; a quantity of unwashed dishes on another; but silence everywhere announced that the hands which should have been busy with all these matters were no longer within reach of them. Mrs. Laval went upstairs again.

" Every creature is gone," she said. " I am sure I do not know what we are to do. *Jealousy*, Norton, did you say ? "

" Because you have sent for these Swiss people, mamma."

" Is it possible ? Well — I don't know what we are to do, as I said. We shall have no dinner."

" I can get the dinner," said Matilda. At which there was some laughing; and then Mrs. Laval said she must go and see how the sick people were. Norton was despatched to find some oysters if he could; and Matilda quietly went downstairs again, with her little head full. She was there still an hour later, when Mrs. Laval came home and called for her. Matilda came running up, with red cheeks.

" Ah, there you are !　What are you doing, Matilda? you have got your face. all flushed."

" It's just the fire," said Matilda.

" Fire?　What are you doing, child ? "

" Nothing, much.　Only trying to put things a little in order."

" *You*," said Mrs. Laval.　" Leave that, my darling.　You cannot.　There will be somebody to do it by and by.　But I wish I had somebody here now, to make gruel, or porridge, or something, for those poor people. They are without any comforts."

Mrs. Laval looked puzzled.

" Are they better ? " Matilda asked.

" Two of them are sick ; indeed they are all sick, more or less ; but the men are really ill, I think."

" If I had some meal, I could make gruel," said Matilda.　" I know how.　I have made it for — I have made it at home, often."

. " Could you ? " said Mrs. Laval.　" There must be some meal here somewhere."

She went down to search for it. But it was found presently that she did not know meal when she saw it; and Matilda's help was needed to decide which barrel held the article.

"I am a useless creature," Mrs. Laval said, as she watched Matilda getting some meal out. "If you can manage that, darling, I will be forever obliged to you, and so will those poor people. It is really good to know how to do things. Why, what have you done with all the dishes and irons that were standing about here? You have got the place in order, I declare! What have you done with them, dear?"

"They are put away. Shall I put on a pot and boil some potatoes, Mrs. Laval? I can; and there is a great piece of cold beef in the pantry."

"Boil potatoes? no, indeed!" said Mrs. Laval. "Norton will get us some oysters, and some bread and some cake at the baker's. No, dear, do not touch the horrid things; keep your hands away from them. We'll fast, for a day or two, and enjoy eating all the better afterwards."

Matilda made her gruel, nicely; and Mrs. Laval carried it herself down to the farm-house. She came back looking troubled. They could not touch it, she said, after all; not one of them but the young girl; they were really a sick house down there; and she would go to New York and get help to-morrow. So by the early morning train she went.

It was rather a day of amusement to the two children left alone at home. They had a great sense of importance upon them, and some sense of business. Matilda at least found a good deal for herself to do, upstairs and downstairs; then she and Norton sat down on the verandah in the soft October light, and consulted over all the details of the tulip and hyacinth beds.

"Fifty dollars!" said Matilda at last.

"Yes?" said Norton. "Well?"   . . ...

"Nothing. Only — did you ever think, Norton, how many other things one could do with fifty dollars? I wonder if it is right to spend so much just on a flower bed?"

"It isn't. It's on two flower beds," said Norton.

"Well, on two. It is the same thing."

"That's a very loose way of talking," said Norton. "Two and one are not at all the same thing. They are three."

"O Norton! but you are twisting things all round, now. I didn't say anything ridiculous."

"I am not so sure of that. Pink, one would never spend money any way, if one stopped because one could spend it some other way."

"But it ought to be always the best way."

"You can't tell what the best way is," said Norton. "I can't think of anything so good to do with this fifty dollars, as to make those two beds of bulbous roots."

Matilda sat thinking, not convinced, but longing very much to see the hyacinths and tulips, when a voice at the glass door behind her made her start.   It was the doctor.

"Good morning.   Is nobody at home?"

"Nobody but us," said Norton.

"Mrs. Laval gone out, eh?"

"Gone to New York, sir."

"To New York, eh? . Ah!   Well!   Unfortunate!"

"What shall I tell her, sir, when she comes back?"

"Is there anybody in the house that can make beef tea?"

"No, sir," said Norton.

"If you will tell me how, Dr. Bird, I will have some," Matilda said.

"You, eh?   Well, you do know something more than most girls.   You can remember and follow directions, if I tell you, eh?"

"Yes, sir.   I think I can."

"Then I'll tell you.   You take a piece of juicy beef—he can see to that—juicy beef;

not a poor cut, mind, nor fat; mustn't be any fat; and you cut it into dice; and when you have cut it all up fine, you put it in a bottle and cork it up. Understand?"

"Yes, sir. But I don't know what dice are."

"Don't, eh? well, little bits as big as the end of my finger, will do as well as dice. Then when you have got your bottle corked, set it in a pot of water, and put the pot on the fire, and let it boil, till the juice of the beef comes out. Then strain that juice. That's beef tea."

"I mustn't put any water in with the beef, sir? — in the bottle?"

"Not a drop. Keep the water all in the pot."

"Who is to have the beef tea, doctor, when it is made?"

"Those two Frenchmen at the farmhouse. I told the women. They ought to have it now. And a nurse too; the women are sick themselves."

Dr. Bird went his way, and Matilda persuaded Norton to go at once in quest of some juicy beef. It would be a difficult job, he said, for the butchers' shops were shut up; but he would go and try. While he was gone, Matilda amused herself with getting a dinner for him and herself down in the kitchen; and there, when he came back, the two went, to eat their dinner and to set the beef tea a going. They had rather a jolly time of it, to tell the truth; and were so very social and discussed so many things besides their beef and bread, that the beef tea was ready to strain by the time Matilda had cleared the things away. And then she and Norton went down to the farmhouse to carry it.

They could get nobody to come to the door, so they opened it for themselves. It was a sad house to see. In two rooms all the family were gathered; the men lying on beds in the inner room, one woman on the floor of the other, and one on a cot. All sick.

The girl alone held her head up; and she complained it was hard to do even that. Matilda and Norton went from one room to another. The men lay like logs, stupid with fever; one of the women was light-headed; not any of them would touch what Matilda had brought. The poor girl who was still on her feet was crying. There was no fire, no friend; no comfort or help of any sort. Norton and his little companion made the rounds helplessly, and then went out to consult together.

"Norton, they are dreadfully sick," whispered Matilda. "I know they are."

"I guess you are right," said Norton. "But you and I can't do anything."

"I can," said Matilda. "I can give them water, and I can give them beef tea. And you, Norton, I will tell you what you can do. Go for Miss Redwood."

"Miss Redwood? who's she?"

"Don't you remember? Mr. Richmond's housekeeper. She'll come, I know."

"She'll be very good if she does," said Norton. "But I'll tell her you said so. Do you think she would come?"

"I'm certain of it."

CHAPTER XI.

NORTON made his way to the brown door of the parsonage, and knocked but the person that opened it was the minister himself. Norton was a little confused now, remembering what his errand meant there.

"Norton Laval, isn't it?" said Mr. Richmond. "You are very welcome, Norton, at my house. Will you come in?"

"No, sir. If you please" —

"What is it? Something you would rather say to me here?"

"No, sir. I was coming" —

"To see me, I hope?"

"No, sir," said Norton, growing desperate and colouring, which he was very unapt to do. "If you please, Mr. Richmond, I was sent to speak to — I forget what her name is — the woman who lives here."

" Miss Redwood ? "

" Yes, sir."

" Who sent you ? "

" Matilda Englefield."

" Did she!   Pray why did not Matilda come with you ? "

" She could not, sir; she was very busy. She asked me to come."

" You can see Miss Redwood," said Mr. Richmond smiling.   " I believe she is always ready to receive visiters; at least I never saw a time when she was not.   You have only to walk right in and knock at her door there. When are you coming to see *me*, Norton ? You and I ought to be better friends."

" I don't know, sir," said Norton.   " I would not intrude."

" Ask your friend ·Matilda if I do not like such intrusions.   I shall have to invite you specially, I see.   Well. go in and find Miss Redwood.   I will not detain you now."

Norton went in, glad to be released, for he did not exactly want to tell his errand to the minister; knocked at the kitchen door and was bade to enter. It was full, the kitchen was, of the sweet smell of baking bread; and Miss Redwood was busily peering into her stove oven.

" Who's there ? " she asked, too much engaged in turning her loaves to give her eyes to anything else, even a visiter. Norton told his name, and waited till the oven doors. shut to with a clang; and then Miss Redwood, very pink in the face, rose up to look at him.

" I've seen you before," was her remark.

" Yes. I brought Matilda Englefield here one day," Norton answered.

" Hm. I thought she brought you. What brings you now ? "

" Matilda wanted me to come with a message to you."

" Well you can sit down and tell it, if you're a mind to. Why didn't the child

come herself? that's the first idee that comes
to me."

" She is busy trying to nurse some sick
folks, and they are more than she can manage; and she wants your help.   At least she
sent me to ask you if you wouldn't come."

" Who's sick? "

" Some people just come from Switzerland
to be my mother's servants."

" Switzerland," repeated Miss Redwood.
" I have heard o' Switzerland, more than
once in my life.   I should like to know
whereabouts it is.   I never knew any one
yet that could tell me."

" Mr. Richmond knows, I suppose," said
Norton.

" I suppose he knows Greek," said Miss
Redwood, " and ever so many other queer
tongues too, I've no doubt; but I should like
to see myself askin' him to learn me.   No, I
mean, as I never knew nobody that I'd ask.
La! there's folks enough that knows.   Only I
never had no chances for them things."

"I could shew you where Switzerland is, if you had a map," said Norton.

"I guess I know as much as that myself," said the housekeeper quietly, opening the stove door again for a peep at the oven. "But what does *that* tell me? I see a little spot o' paper painted green, and a big spot along side of it painted some other colour; and the map is all spots; and somebody tells me that little green spot is Switzerland. And I should like to know, how much wiser am I for that? That's paper and green paint; but what I want to know is, where is the *place?*"

"It's hard to tell," said Norton, so much amused that he forgot his commission.

"Well, these folks come from Switzerland, you say. How did they come?"

"They came in a ship — part of the way."

"How fur in a ship?"

"Three thousand miles."

"Three thousand," repeated Miss Redwood. "When you get up there, I don't know what miles mean, no more than if you spoke another language. I understand a hundred miles. It's nigh that to New York."

" They came that hundred miles, over and above," said Norton.

" Well, how long now, does it take a ship to go that fur? Three thousand miles."

" It depends on how fast the wind blows."

" The wind goes awful fast sometimes," said Miss Redwood. " When it goes at that rate as will carry a chimney off a house, and pick up a tree by the roots as I would a baby under my arm, seems to me a ship would travel at a powerful speed."

" It would certainly, if there was nothing to hinder," said Norton; " but at those times, you see, the wind picks up the water, and sends such huge waves rolling about that it is not very safe to be where they can give you a slap. Ships don't get along best at such times."

" Well, I'm thankful I'm not a sailor," said Miss Redwood. " I'd rather stay home and know less. How many o' these folks o' yourn is sick?"

"All of them, pretty much," said Norton. "Two men and two women."

"Fever nagur?"

"No, 'tisn't that. I don't know what it is. The doctor is attending them. He ordered beef tea to-day; and Matilda made some; but they seem too sick to take it now they've got it."

Miss Redwood dropped her towel, with which she was just going to open the oven again, and stood upright.

"Beef tea?" she echoed. "How long have these folks been sick?"

"Ever since they came ashore almost. They came straight up here, and began to be ill immediately. That was a few days ago; not a week."

"Beef tea!" said Miss Redwood again. "And just come to shore. How do they look? Did you see them?"

"Yes, I saw them," said Norton. "I went

with Matilda when she took the beef tea to them. How did they look? I can't tell; they looked bad. The men were mahogany colour; and one of the women was out of her head, I think."

" And you two children going to see them!" exclaimed Miss Redwood, in a tone that savoured of strong disapprobation, not to say dismay.

" Because there was no one else," said Norton. " Mamma has gone to New York to get more people; for all ours went off when they knew of the sickness at the farmhouse."

" Why?" said Miss Redwood sharply.

" I don't know. I suppose they were jealous of these strangers."

" Hm," said Miss Redwood, beginning now to take her bread out of the oven with a very hurried hand; " there's jealousy enough in the world, no doubt, and unreason enough; but it don't usually come like an epidemic neither. You go home, and tell Matilda I'm a comin' as fast as ever I kin get my chores

done and my hood and shawl on. And you
tell her — will she do what you tell her?"

"I don't know," said Norton. "What is
it?"

"*Where* is it these folks are sick? Not to
your house?"

"O no. Down at the farmhouse — you
know our farmhouse — under the bank."

"Did you leave the child there?"

"She was there when I came away."

"Well, you run home as fast as your legs
can carry you and fetch her out of that.
Bring her home, and don't you nor she go
down there again. Maybe it's no harm, but
it's safe to do as I tell you. Now go, and
I'll come. Don't let the grass grow under
your feet."

Norton was not used to be ordered about
quite so decidedly; it struck him as an amusing variety in his life. However he divined
that Miss Redwood might have some deep
reason for being so energetic, and he was not
slow in getting back to Briery Bank; so his

mother's place was called. The house was shut up, as he and Matilda had left it; and he went on down to the home of the sick people. There he found Matilda as he had left her. Norton only put his head into the sick room and called her out.

"Miss Redwood is coming," he said.

"I'm so glad! I knew she would," said Matilda. "She will know what to do. They all seem stupid, Norton, except the woman who is out of her head."

"Yes, she will know what to do," said Norton; "and you had better come away now. You don't."

"I can do something, though," said Matilda. "I can give the medicine and the beef tea. Why there was nobody even to give the medicine, Norton. I found it here with the doctor's directions; and nobody had taken it till I came; not one of these sick people. But oh, the rooms are so disagreeable, with so many sick people in them! you can't think."

" I can, for I've been in them," said Norton. " And once is enough. They have got the medicine now, Pink; you needn't stay any longer."

" O yes, but I must. I must till Miss Redwood comes. The medicine will have to be taken again in a little while."

" It can wait till she gets here. You come away, Pink. Miss Redwood said you should."

" She didn't know what there was for me to do, or she wouldn't have said it. I can't go, Norton."

" But you *must*, Pink. She said so. Suppose these people should be sick with something dreadful? you can't tell."

" I am sure they would want a nurse then."

" But *you* might get sick, you know."

" Well, Norton, I'm not afraid."

" You might get sick, all the same, if you're *not* afraid," said Norton impatiently. " Come, Pink, you must come."

"I can't, Norton. I must go in and give them some more beef tea, now in a minute. They can't take but ever so little at a time. It would be very wrong to leave them as they are."

"You might get sick, and die," said Norton.

"Well, Norton," said Matilda slowly, "I don't think I am afraid of that. I belong to Jesus. He will take care of me."

"I don't think you know what you are talking of!" said Norton, very impatient and very much at a loss how to manage Matilda.

"O yes, I do!" she said smiling. "Now I must go in. *You* needn't come, for there wouldn't be anything for you to do."

Matilda disappeared; and Norton, wishing very much that he could lay hold of her and carry her away by force, did not however feel that it would exactly do. He sat down on the door stone of the house, he would not go further, and waited. There was a delicious calm sunlight over all the world that October afternoon; it puzzled Norton how there could be a sick house anywhere under such a sky. He heard the ponies stamping their idle hoofs against the barn floor; they were spoiling for exercise; why were he and Matilda not out driving, instead of having this state of things? Then some gayly disposed crows went flying overhead, calling a cheery reminder to each other as they went along; *they* were having a good time. Norton chafed against the barriers that hindered him. Suddenly a swift footstep came over the grass, and Mr. Richmond stood before him.

"Is this the house?" he asked. "Is Matilda here?"

"Yes, sir; and I've tried to get her out, and I can't."

Mr. Richmond went in, without more words. A moment after, Matilda opened the door he had shut.

"Well! will you go now?" said Norton.

"I must. Mr. Richmond will not let me stay."

Mr. Richmond himself came again to the door.

" Norton," said he, " I am going to ask you to take Matilda to the parsonage. The best thing will be for you and her to make your home there, until Mrs. Laval gives further orders. You will both be heartily welcome. Will you take her there and take care of her until I come home?"

" Thank you, sir," said Norton, " it is not necessary " —

" You must let my word go for that," said the minister smiling. " If not necessary, I think it prudent. I wish it; and I invite both of you. It would be treating me very ill to refuse me, and I am sure you will not do that. I trust you to take care of Matilda until I get home. The house will be quite alone when Miss Redwood leaves it. Is anybody in the house on the bank?"

" No, sir; nobody."

" I will lock it up, then, and bring the key. Go in and put up anything you will want for a day or two, and I will send it after you."

With a nod and a smile at them, Mr. Richmond went in again. The two children looked at each other, and then began to mount the bank.

" You do what Mr. Richmond tells you," remarked Norton.

" Of course," said Matilda. " So do you."

" It wouldn't be civil to do anything else," said Norton. " But isn't it jolly, that you and I should go to make a visit at the parsonage! What is a parsonage like? It isn't like other houses, I suppose."

" Why yes, it is," said Matilda; " just like; only a minister lives in it."

" That makes the difference," said Norton. " Don't you feel as if you were in church all the time? I shall, I know."

" Why no, Norton! what an idea. Mr. Richmond's house is not like a church."

" Isn't he like a minister? "

" Why yes, of course!" said Matilda with

some indignation. " He isn't like *your* minister, Norton."

" Why ? " said Norton laughing.

" I don't know. He isn't stiff. He don't dress unlike other people. He is just as pleasant as anybody else can be; and a *great* deal pleasanter, I think."

" What you call good people, generally are stiff," said Norton.

" O no, Norton, they are not. What makes you think so ? "

" You were very stiff just now," said Norton.

" O, do you mean *that* sort of stiffness? But Norton, I thought there was something I could do there, you know, and I didn't think I ought to come away."

Getting to the top of the bank broke off the discussion. Matilda and Norton each had things to get together to go to the parsonage; and it was necessary to change their dress. The sun was well on his westing way when they left the iron gate of Briery Bank, bag in

hand; and in the little lane of the parsonage
the elm trees cast broad and long shadows.
As they came up on the piazza, Miss Redwood opened the door. Her hood and shawl
were on, and she had a basket in her hand.
She stopped suddenly.

"What is it now?" she said. "What's
wanting?"

"Nothing," said Matilda; "only Mr. Richmond has sent us here."

"He has!" said the housekeeper. "You've
come to stop?"

"Mr. Richmond says so.   He wished it."

"Well, what 'll you do?" said Miss Redwood coming to a sort of pause. "There
ain't a living soul in the house, and there
won't be; 'cept the minister himself; and
how he'll get along I don't know.   I can't be
in two places at once."

"Can't I get the tea, Miss Redwood?"

"La, I don't know but what you kin.
Come along in, and let me tell you.   There's
bread all baked, this afternoon — it ain't cold

yet — enough to last a siege; it's in that pantry, Matilda, in the bread box. You know there's all the cups and saucers and tea things, for you've seen me get 'em out; and the tea canister; and the sugar. And the milk is down cellar, in a pan, and there's cream onto it. Can you skim it off and keep it cream yet, for the minister's tea?"

" O yes; I can do that, Miss Redwood."

" Then you'll get along for to-night; and I'll try and be round in the morning, if I kin. But you'll want sheets — There's the bed in the spare room off the hall; that's all ready for one of ye; I got it fixed up Saturday for somebody that never come; 'tain't everybody as sticks to his word like the minister. La, I get weary with the folks that are like Job's brooks; they say and don't do; and when you expect 'em they ain't there. I was put out, o' Saturday, when I found out that was how it was with this man; but there's good in everything, if you can keep your patience; now the room's ready, and it wouldn't ha' been ready; for I had a lot o' apples there dryin', and a board full o' fresh turnpikes was on the bed; *they* was gettin' finished; and I had a quilt in a corner that I had sot up on the sticks and it was a'most done quiltin'; and all them things I had to fly round and get rid of; and I've no time for anything now. So dear, that room 'll do for one of ye; and the other — you can put the sheets on the bed, can't ye? for the minister 'll be playin' nurse till I come, and I wish I had Jack's seven-mile boots to get to Briery Bank with."

While this talk was going on, Miss Redwood had brought Matilda upstairs, and was taking out linen and coverlets from a press in one of the rooms. Matilda said she could manage everything, with Norton's help.

"Then I'll go," said Miss Redwood. "But if I shouldn't be able fur to run away in the morning and see to the breakfast!" —

She stopped, thinking.

"Dear Miss Redwood, won't you trust me to do it? I think I can."

" What sort of a breakfast will it be ? " said the housekeeper meditatively.

" I'll *try* to have it right."

" La, yes, if it depended on your tryin'," said the housekeeper; " your will is as good as gold; but *will* won't cook a beefsteak."

" I'll try," said Matilda again.

" Well," said Miss Redwood, " we must walk till we get out o' the woods, and then we'll run.   The minister ain't accustomed to have his steak any way but as he likes it; maybe it'll do him no harm.   Everything's down cellar, Matilda, 'cept the things in the kitchen pantry; and you'll find out which is which.   And I'll go."

So she did.   And as the door closed after her, the two children in the hall looked at each other.

" Nobody in the house ? " said Norton.

" Nobody but ourselves."

" That's jolly," said Norton.   " Pink, I have got that catalogue in my pocket; let us sit down somewhere and make out a list of those hyacinths."

" O Norton ! — Yes, I will in a little while. I must go get the table ready for tea ; and I had better do it now before Mr. Richmond comes home."

" You and I seem to have a great deal of getting tea to do," said Norton, as he followed Matilda into the little dining room. " What do you want *me* to do ? "

" O Norton ! — if you would just look and see if the tea-kettle is on, and if not, put it on. Will you ? "

" Where, Pink ? "

" Just open that door. There is the kitchen."

" I remember," said Norton. " No, the kettle isn't on. Here goes."

There was a little busy, pleasant bustle, for a time; and then Matilda with Norton's help had got everything in order for the evening meal. The sun was near setting, and threw bright lines of light in at the two little west windows, filling the small dining room with pure gold ; then it went down, and the gold was gone, and only in the low western sky the brightness remained.

"It's time for the minister to be at home," Norton said.

"He has a great deal to do," Matilda answered.

"What?" said Norton. "I always thought the parsons had an easy time of it. I could write two themes a week, I think, if I tried hard."

"Norton!" Matilda exclaimed, "it isn't that; and Mr. Richmond doesn't write themes, as you call it, to begin with."

"That must be harder then," said Norton; "to stand up and speak to people without anything to say."

"Why he doesn't!" said Matilda. "Mr. Richmond always has plenty to say. I suppose he could talk all day, if he didn't get tired."

"I mean preaching," said Norton.

"Yes, and I mean preaching," said Matilda.

"Where is it to come from?" said the boy, pursing his lips ready for a whistle.

"Why, out of his head, and out of his heart," said Matilda. "Where should it come from?"

"I say, Pink," said Norton, "it's very funny for me to be here. I don't think I can stand it long."

"Stand what?"

"This. Being at the parsonage, and getting talked to. I suppose I shall."

"Norton," said Matilda confidently, "you'll like it. It's just nice."

"I don't know about that," said Norton. "It feels queer. I believe I am afraid."

Matilda laughed at his very un-fear-like face; and then the front door opened and shut. Mr. Richmond had come.

It was a jolly tea they had, Norton confessed afterwards. Mr. Richmond went rummaging among Miss Redwood's stores and brought out a jar of sweetmeats; in honour, he said, of his guests. The sweetmeats were

good, and so was Miss Redwood's fresh bread.
And there was indeed plenty of talk at the
table; but it was not in the least like preaching. From the sick Swiss, and their voyage,
Mr. Richmond and Norton somehow got
upon the subject of navigation, and commerce,
with ships ancient and modern, and a little
touch here and there shewing how much these
things have had to do with the history of the
world and the life of nations. Mr. Richmond
and Norton talked and talked; and Matilda
listened, and made the tea, and enjoyed it all
very much, seeing too what a good time Norton was having.

After tea, they removed into the study.
Mr. Richmond asked them to come there, saying he was going to play this evening. He
built up a beautiful fire, and gave Norton a
book to look at; while he himself sat for
awhile quite silent, looking into the blaze, and
only moving now and then to take care that
it was kept up. So Matilda found the two,
when she had put the tea things away and

followed them to the study. The red curtains were drawn across the windows, the red light of the fire leaped and shone all through the room; in the glow of it Norton sat brooding over his book, and before it Mr. Richmond sat thinking. But he held out his hand as Matilda came in, and asked if his little house-keeper had got all things straight. Matilda came to his outstretched hand, which drew her to his side; and the room was still again. Matilda stood motionless. By and by Norton glanced up at her from his book, and covertly smiled. It started Matilda's thoughts.

"Are you not going to be busy, Mr. Richmond?" she ventured gently.

"Not doing anything at all," said Mr. Richmond rousing himself. "I have been busy all day, Matilda. I am going to do nothing to-night. What is it?"

"Will it be doing anything, to talk to Norton and me?"

"I can't say," Mr. Richmond replied, laughing a little. "Perhaps you will find me work to do, but I'll risk it.   What do you want to talk about?"

"There was a question — Norton and I could not tell what the answer ought to be. I believe he thought one way, and I thought another."

"What was the question?" said Mr. Richmond; while Norton's face looked up from his book, bright with the same query.

"We were talking — it was about opportunities, you know, Mr. Richmond; the opportunities that having money gives people; and we couldn't tell, Norton and I, how far one ought to go.   Norton said people must stop somewhere; and I suppose they must. Where ought they to stop?"

Matilda's face looked very earnest.   Norton's, comical.

"Where ought they to stop in giving money, you mean?"

"Yes, sir.   For doing good, you know, and making other people comfortable."

"It is rather a large question.   Were you

afraid of giving too much, or of giving too little?"

"I think one of us was afraid of giving too much, and the other of giving too little."

"The best way is to go to the Bible and see what that says. May I trouble one of you to open it at the second epistle to the Corinthians, and read what you find in the seventh verse of the ninth chapter?"

Norton dropped his book and sprang to do the service asked for. He read the words, —

"'Every man according as he purposeth in his heart, so let him give; not grudgingly, or of necessity: for God loveth a cheerful giver.'"

Norton read, and looked up, as much as to say, What now? how does this help?

"I don't see how that tells, Mr. Richmond," said Matilda.

"It tells one or two things. You are to give out of your heart; not because somebody else asks you, or some other body says you ought. *That* would not please God. You are to do what you *like* to do; much or little, as you feel."

"But ought it to be much or little?"

"As you feel. As your heart says."

"But then, Mr. Richmond, will the Lord be just as well pleased whether it is much or little?"

"Norton will please read the sixth verse."

"'But this I say, He which soweth sparingly shall reap also sparingly; and he which soweth bountifully shall reap also bountifully.'"

"But that don't tell either," said Norton, when he had read.

"I think it does," said Matilda slowly. "It tells one thing. Mr. Richmond, it doesn't tell *how much* one ought to like to give. That was the very question between Norton and me; and we could not settle it."

"Don't you see, Matilda, that everybody's heart would give its own answer to that question?"

"But Mr. Richmond, surely there is a right and a wrong answer?"

"I am afraid, a good many wrong answers," said Mr. Richmond.

Norton looked as if he would like to say something, but modestly kept back before the minister. Mr. Richmond caught the look.

"Speak out, Norton," said he smiling. "Truth will always bear to be looked at."

"I don't know much about it, sir," said Norton. "Only it seems to me, that if one begins to help other people all one can, one will soon want helping himself."

"Ah!" said Mr. Richmond. "Read the next verse now."

"The next to the seventh, sir?—'And God is able to make all grace abound toward you; that ye, always having all sufficiency in all things, may abound to every good work.'"

"That does not sound as if Matilda were in any danger of growing poor through helping Mrs. Eldridge,—does it?"

" But sir ! " said Norton, — " the more one gives away, the less one has for oneself ? "

" It does not always work so," said Mr. Richmond. " The Bible says, ' There is that scattereth, and yet increaseth.' "

Norton did not know exactly how to fight for his opinions, and so was silent, like a well-bred boy as he was; but Matilda's feeling was different.

" I understand," she said ; " at least I think I do; but Mr. Richmond, this does not get Norton and me out of our puzzle. You don't mean, that people ought to keep nothing for themselves ? "

" ' Every man according as he purposeth in his heart,' " Mr. Richmond repeated. " That is the order. There have been people, Matilda, who have given their all for the sake of the Lord Jesus, and kept, as you say, nothing for themselves. It was in their heart. I cannot blame them, for one. He did not."

" But ought every one to do so ? "

" Matilda, I dare not set any rule but the

rule my Master has set.   *He* said, — ' He that forsaketh not all that he hath, he cannot be my disciple.' "

" People don't do that, sir," said Norton eagerly.

" *Ought* they to do it, sir ? " said Matilda timidly.   " To give away all they have got ? "

" He did not say, ' give away,' but ' forsake.' The word means literally ' to take leave of.' They give up thinking that what they have is their own ; and from that time stand ready to give it away entirely, if the Master says so."

" Is that religion, sir ? " Norton asked.

" But, Mr. Richmond," Matilda said in another tone, " that is the very thing.   How are they to know when he does tell them to give these things away ? "

" We are coming to it now," said Mr. Richmond.   " You want to know what religion is, Norton.   Please turn to the fifth chapter of that same epistle to the Corinthians, and read aloud the — let me see, — I think it is the fourteenth and fifteenth verses."

Norton obeyed.

"'For the love of Christ constraineth us; because we thus judge, that if one died for all, then were all dead: and that he died for all, that they which live should not henceforth live unto themselves; but unto him which died for them and rose again.'"

"That is your answer," said Mr. Richmond; "that is religion. Now for Matilda's answer — Norton, turn to the epistle to the Colossians, and the third chapter, and read the seventeenth verse."

·"'And whatsoever ye do, in word or deed, do all in the name of the Lord Jesus, giving thanks to God and the Father, by him.'"

"There is your rule, Matilda. It is carrying out the former words. You have only to apply that to everything you do."

"What is doing all .*in the name* of the Lord?" Norton asked.

"Not in your own name; not as though you were your own master; not as seeking first your own pleasure or advancement; not as using your own things. Correlatively, for the Lord; for his pleasure, for his service, as belonging to him."

" 'In word or deed,' " said Matilda. " That means giving and everything."

" But then, in religion one would never be free," said Norton.

" How, never be free?"

" Why one must act as if one never belonged to oneself."

" We don't," said Mr. Richmond. " We are *not* our own ; we are bought with a price. And we never were free till now."

" But if I go to buy a coat " — said Norton ; and he stopped.

" Yes, if you go to buy a coat; you will remember that you and the coat are the Lord's together ; and you will buy that coat which you think is the one he would like you to wear, and in which you can best work for him ; and not use his money for any other."

Norton was silent, not because he had no thoughts to speak. Matilda was silent, but with a very different face. It was serious, sweet, meditative, and content.

"I see how it is, Mr. Richmond," she said at last, looking up to his face. "Thank you, sir."

"It is very nice to have people apply sermons for themselves, Matilda," said the minister.

CHAPTER XII.

MISS REDWOOD did not come back the next morning to get breakfast. No sign of her. Mr. Richmond and Matilda managed it, between them. Norton, I am afraid, was not up till Matilda called him, and that was when the coffee was nearly ready.

Matilda learned how to get breakfast at the parsonage, and Norton learned to be up and help her; for they made a long stay at the old brown house. Mrs. Laval's Swiss servants were all down with ship fever; and the two children were forbidden to come even near the house. Mrs. Laval herself staid at home and did what she could for the sufferers; but she and Miss Redwood kept house alone together. Not a servant would be hired to come within reach of the dreadful contagion; and not a friend thought it was any use to go there just then to see anybody. Mrs. Laval and Miss Redwood had it all to themselves, with no one to look at besides but Mr. Richmond and the doctor. Mr. Richmond came to them constantly.

The flow of human sympathy went all to the house with the brown door. It was remarkable, how many friends were eager to know how the children got on; and how many more were anxious to be allowed to come in to help Matilda.

"What shall I do, Mr. Richmond?" she would say. "There have been three this morning."

"Who were they, Tilly?"

"Mrs. Barth, and Miss Van Dyke, and Miss Spenser,— O there were four!—and Ailie Swan."

"Do you want Ailie to help you?"

"No, Mr. Richmond; I don't want anybody, but Norton."

"Well, I don't. You may tell them that

we do not want anybody, Matilda. I have seen Mrs. Pottenburg. She will come in to scrub floors and do the hard work."

So for several weeks the two children and the minister kept house together; in a way highly enjoyed by Matilda, and I think by Mr. Richmond too. Even Norton found it oddly pleasant, and got very fond of Mr. Richmond; who he declared privately to Matilda was a brick of the right sort. All the while the poor Swiss people at Mrs. Laval's farmhouse were struggling for life, and their two nurses led a weary, lonely existence. Norton sometimes wished he and Matilda could get at the grey ponies and have a good drive; but Matilda did not care about it. She would rather not be seen out of doors. As the weeks went on, she was greatly afraid that her aunt would come back and reclaim her.

And Mrs. Candy did come back; and meeting Mr. Richmond a day or two after her return, she desired that he would send Matilda home to her. She had just learned where she was, she said.

" You know that Matilda has been exposed to ship fever ? " said Mr. Richmond.

" No. I heard she was at your house."

" But not until she had been in the house with the fever patients, and nursing them, before any one knew what was the matter. Had she not better stay where she is, at least until we can be certain that she has got no harm ? "

" Well, perhaps," said Mrs. Candy, looking confused ; — " it is very perplexing ; I cannot expose my daughter " —

" She will stay where she is," said Mr. Richmond, " for the present. Good morning."

He never told Matilda of this encounter. And before another week had gone, Mrs. Candy and Clarissa had again left Shady-walk.

So week after week went by peacefully. The beautiful days of October were all past; November winds came, and the trees were bare, and the frosts at night began to be severe. The sick people were getting better, and terrible qualms of fear and sorrow now and then swept over Matilda's heart. Her aunt would surely want her back now, and she should never finish her visit at Mrs. Laval's!

One day she was in Mr. Richmond's study, all alone, thinking so. There was a flurry of snow in the air, the first snow of the season; falling thickly on the grass, and eddying in windy circles through the pine trees. Matilda had knelt in a chair at the window to watch it, with that spasm of fear at her heart. Now it is winter! she thought. Aunt Candy *must* be home soon. Yet the whirling great flakes of snow were so lovely, that in a few minutes they half distracted her from her fear.

It came back again, when she saw Mr. Richmond appear from the end of the church porch and make his way across the snow towards the parsonage door. Matilda watched him lovingly; then was possessed with a sudden notion that he was bringing her news. He walks as if he had something to say, she said to herself; and he will come in and say it.

He came in and warmed his hands at the fire, without sitting down; certainly there *was* an air of business about him, as she had thought. Matilda stood watching and waiting; that fear at her heart.

"Where's Norton?" said Mr. Richmond.

"He went out a good while ago. I don't know, sir."

"I suppose you have expected to hear of your aunt's coming home, before now, Matilda?"

"Yes, sir," said the child. He watched her furtively. No curiosity, no question; her face settled rather into a non-expectant state, as if all were fixed for her for ever. A look Mr. Richmond did not like to see.

"She has come home."

He saw the colour flit on Matilda's cheek; her mouth had quitted its lines of peace and gayety and become firm; she said nothing.

"You are not glad to hear of it, Matilda."

"No, sir."

"It is no pleasure to tell you of it; but it is necessary. How do you feel towards her now?"

"Mr. Richmond," said the child slowly, "I think — I don't hate her any more."

"But you would like to be excused from living with her?"

Matilda did not reply; no answer was necessary to so self-evident a proposition; the child seemed to be gathering her forces, somehow, mentally.

"Take courage," said her friend. "I have concluded that you never shall live with her any more. That is at an end."

He saw the lightning flash of delight come into Matilda's eyes; a streak of red shewed itself on her cheek; but she was breathless, waiting for more words to make her understand how this could be, or that she had heard right.

"It's true," said Mr. Richmond.

"But — how then?" said Matilda.

"Mrs. Laval wants you."

" Wants me ? " — Matilda repeated anxiously.

" She wants you, to keep you for her own child.   She lost a little daughter once.   She wants you to be in that little daughter's place, and to live with her always."

" But, aunt Candy will not," — said Matilda, " she will not " —

· " Your aunt Candy has consented.   I have arranged that.   It is safely done, Matilda. You are to live with Mrs. Laval and be her child from henceforth."

Matilda still looked at Mr. Richmond for a minute or two, as if there must be words to follow that would undo the wonderful tale of these; but seeing that Mr. Richmond only smiled, there came a great change over the child's face.   The fixedness broke up.   Yet she did not smile; she seemed for the instant to grow grave and old; and clasping her little hands, she turned away from Mr. Richmond and walked the breadth of the room and back.

Then she stood still again beside the table, sober and pale. She looked at Mr. Richmond, waiting to hear more.

"It is all true," said her friend.

"Is it for *always?*" Matilda asked in a low voice.

"Yes. Even so. Mrs. Laval was very earnest in wishing it. I judged you would not be unwilling, Matilda."

The child said nothing, but the streak of colour began again to come into her cheeks.

"You are now to be Mrs. Laval's child. She adopts you for her own. In all respects, except that of memory, you are to be as if you had been born hers."

"Does Norton know?"

"I have not spoken to him. I really cannot tell."

Again silence fell. Matilda stood with her eyes downcast, the colour deepening in each cheek. Mr. Richmond watched her.

"Have I done right?" he asked.

"You, sir?" said Matilda looking up.

" Yes.   Have I done right?   I have made
no mistake for your happiness ? "

" Did *you* do it, sir ? "

" Yes, in one way.   Mrs. Laval wished it;
I arranged it.   You know your mother left
me the power.   Have I done right? "

" Mr. Richmond," said the child slowly, " I
am afraid to think."

Her friend smiled again, and waited till the
power of speech should come back.

" Was aunt Candy willing? " she said
then.

" No, I do not think she was willing.   I
think the plan was not agreeable to her.   But
she gave her consent to it.   The reasons in
favour of the plan were so strong that she
could not help that."

Matilda privately wondered that any reasons could have had so much weight; and
rather fancied that Mr. Richmond had been
the strongest reason of them all.

" And it is *all done?* " she said, lifting up
her eyes.

" All done. Arranged and finished. But Mrs. Laval is afraid to have you come home before next week."

" Mr. Richmond," said the child, coming close and stealing her hand into his, " I am very much obliged to you ! "

Her friend sat down and drew his arm around her; and Matilda's other hand on his shoulder, they were both still, thinking, for some little time.

" Mr. Richmond " — Matilda whispered, I think I am somebody else."

" I hope not, Tilly."

" Everything in the world seems different."

" Very naturally; but you can keep yourself yet, I trust. If I thought not, I should wish the whole thing undone."

" I ought to be better " — said Matilda.

" We ought always to be better. Circumstances cannot change that. *Nothing* happens, that the Lord does not mean shall help us to be better. And yet, sometimes circumstances seem to make it more difficult."

" These don't, Mr. Richmond, — do they ? "

" I don't know, Tilly.　They may."

" How ? "

" I will not forestall them, Tilly.　If you watch, you will soon find out, whether they do or not."

" Are you afraid I shall be different, Mr. Richmond ? *not* growing better, I mean."

" I have not seen you tried, except in one way, you know."

" I shall have more opportunities; shall I not, Mr. Richmond ? "

" Different opportunities.　You have had no lack of them so far, have you ? "

" Of one sort, Mr. Richmond."

" Ah, but remember, my child, we are never without opportunities to do the Lord's will; plenty of opportunities.　What you are think-ing of now, is opportunity to do your own will; isn't it ? "

" I was thinking of helping people, and doing things for those who have no money."

" Yes.　And is not that a pleasure ? "

" O yes, sir."

" When the Lord puts it out of our power to have this pleasure, it shews that those things are not his will for us just then ; eh ? " .

" Yes, sir."

" What is our opportunity then ? "

" I know what you mean, Mr. Richmond. You mean, that then we can be patient."

" And content."

" *Content?* "

" Yes; if it is God's will. We must be content always to do that."

" But I suppose," said Matilda, " I *shall*, maybe, have more chance to do those things, Mr. Richmond."

" If so, I hope you will do them. But I want you to be always ready to do all the will of God. It is easy to pick out a pleasant duty here and there, or an unpleasant duty even ; and stand ready to be faithful in that. But I want you to watch and be faithful in all things; that you may prove what is that good and acceptable and perfect will of God."

"I will try, Mr. Richmond."

"In every change of circumstances, Matilda, we find both new opportunities and new difficulties. God has something new for us in every change. The thing is, to be ready for it."

"How can one always find out, Mr. Richmond, what it is?"

"If you watch, and are obedient, the Lord will shew it to you."

Norton's step sounded on the piazza. Mr. Richmond loosened the hold of his arm, and Matilda rushed off. Not so fast but that she stopped midway between him and the door and said, soberly, —

"Thank you, Mr. Richmond. I think I understand. I will try."

THE NEW JUVENILES.

The Bessie Books.

I. BESSIE AT THE SEASIDE. 16mo $1.25

II. BESSIE IN THE CITY, 16mo 1.25

III. BESSIE AND HER FRIENDS. 16mo . . . 1.25

IV. BESSIE AMONG THE MOUNTAINS. 16mo. 1.25

V. BESSIE AT SCHOOL. 16mo 1.25

VI. BESSIE ON HER TRAVELS. (*Preparing.*) . 1.25

"Bessie is a very charming specimen of little girlhood. It is a lovely story of home and nursery life among a family of bright, merry little children." — *Presbyterian.*

Butterfly's Flights.

BY THE AUTHOR OF THE "WIN AND WEAR" SERIES.

Six vols. in a box. $3.60.

I. AT MOUNT MANSFIELD.	IV. AT MONTREAL.
II. AT SARATOGA.	V. AT THE SEA SIDE.
III. AT NIAGARA.	VI. IN PHILADELPHIA.

(*These volumes are not sold separately.*)

HOW JENNIE FOUND HER LORD. By the author of "The Golden Ladder Series." 18mo 0.35

TIBBY THE CHARWOMAN, AND OTHER STORIES.
18mo $0.50

A very charming Scotch story.

Dr. Newton's New Book,

BIBLE WONDERS. By the Rev. Richard Newton,
D.D. 6 illustrations. 16mo 1.25

———

LITTLE EFFIE'S HOME. By the author of "Bertie
Lee," "Donald Fraser," &c. 16mo. 4 fine illustrations 1.25

LITTLE DROPS OF RAIN. By the author of
"Nell's Mission." 16mo. 4 illustrations 1.00

NELL'S MISSION. 18mo 0.50

GRANDFATHER'S NELL. By the author of
"Squire Downing's Heirs." 4 fine illustrations. 16mo 1.25

MARGARET RUSSELL'S SCHOOL. 4 illus. . . 1.25

SQUIRE DOWNING'S HEIRS. 4 illustrations . . 1.25

THE LITTLE PEAT CUTTERS; OR, THE SONG
OF LOVE. By EMMA MARSHALL. 18mo 0.50

TEDDY'S DREAM; OR, A LITTLE SWEEP'S MIS-
SION. By EMMA LESLIE. 18mo 0.50

LITTLE JACK'S FOUR LESSONS. By the author
of "Ellen Montgomery's Bookshelf," &c. 16mo 0.60

HEBREW HEROES. By A. L. O. E. 16mo . 1.50

THE GOLDEN FLEECE. By A. L. O. E. 16mo . 1.00

LITTLE FREDDIE FEEDING HIS SOUL. 18mo 0.50

AUNT MILDRED'S LEGACY. By the author of
"Battles Worth Fighting." 16mo 1.25